DEAD M[...]

BOOKS BY
JOHN BLACKBURN

DEAD MAN RUNNING

BROKEN BOY

A SOUR APPLE TREE

DEAD MAN RUNNING was originally published in hard cover by M. S. Mill Company and William Morrow & Company. Its large sale in the higher priced edition makes possible this inexpensive Lancer reprint.

DEAD MAN RUNNING

JOHN BLACKBURN

LANCER BOOKS • NEW YORK

A LANCER BOOK • 1966

LANCER BOOKS, INC. ° 185 MADISON AVENUE • NEW YORK, N.Y. 10016

CHAPTER ONE

THEY found Susan Carlin beneath the double bed of a week-end cottage, and part of her was still lovely. Her body, for instance, was without flaw and looked as expensive as ever in its Balmain suit, and fifteen-guinea shoes, and a coat that had cost the lives of many small animals. The face was a horror worth nothing at all.

And, outside the cottage, they found the hands of the man who had killed her. Their prints were clear on the wheel of his car, and the gun that had shattered her face, and soon they knew the full story.

They never found the man himself though, and, after a time, they stopped looking. "He's gone away," they said. "He's gone far away where we can never touch him. Yes, this man killed his wife, and then did something worse. Peter Carlin turned traitor and he's dead—he's dead and done with."

The chair stood in a thin pool of Russian sunlight and it was clamped to the floor. The clamps were so arranged that its occupant had to look at Gregor Radek, but Radek didn't look back at him. He was looking at the photographs on the wall.

He looked at the hawks wheeling across the mountain they called Two-Headed Ushba, the deer racing on the frozen tundra, and the big wolf very still and white-eyed in the camera flash. Radek smiled as he looked at those pictures, for they were old friends who gave him strength and comfort and love; far more love than he had ever felt for a human being. Then he turned to the man in the chair and his smile went out.

"Mr. Carlin," said Radek, the man who loved animals. "Mr. Carlin, you have killed your wife, you have betrayed your country, and now—now you have lied to me."

You have killed your wife. Peter Carlin sat quite rigid in his chair, facing forward as the clamps made him, and the words still conveyed nothing at all.

Yet they said he'd killed Susan, and they seemed so certain of it. *You did it*, they said. *You killed her and now you've run away.* He'd heard it all so many times, but the words were just words and didn't mean anything.

Susan was dead enough. She was dead and laid out on the floor of the Sussex cottage, with his prints on the gun that had killed her, and outside, in the shadows, his car had waited, while a plane carried him on towards Russia.

You have betrayed your country. Yes, they probably believed that too now, for he'd had the opportunity and the motive; the opportunity to walk at will through a line of saw-tooth huts where knowledge was made. The knowledge of a steel box containing two yards of wire, a pound of lead, a little glass, and twelve ounces of crystal, copper, and polythene; all common, all cheap materials, but, when arranged in a certain pattern they added up to Zero; the means to take a rocket home.

"No," he said, trying to look past the man at the desk and watch the sun glinting on the dome of the Saint Izac Cathedral. "No, I never lied to you." And, as he spoke, he felt very like that cathedral; an empty shell without hope or purpose. A church with no altar, and where no masses were sung. Where nothing moved, except the pendulum swinging from the roof to prove that Galileo knew the world was round.

"Very well, then it seems I will have to believe you. Very much against my wish I must accept your word. And I am sorry for you, Mr. Carlin, extremely sorry." Radek nodded his head and once more Peter Carlin noted the boredom in his face; boredom and fatigue and complete indifference. The face of an official who did a routine job he was paid to do but kept part of his mind free in a very personal and private world. He had seen Radek each day for a week now and was beginning to understand what that world was.

It was made up of several things and not one of them was human. It was the natural history books on the shelves, the Gould bird plates on the wall behind him and the photographs in front. It was the longed-for months of his holiday when he sat alone and at peace and watched the bears lumbering up the Ural foothills, and eagles wheeling above the Caucasus and the seals playing in the green sea they called "White". It was a little flat in a back street which he shared with two dogs, a Cypriot cat and a tame jackdaw which came and went at will through the ever open window.

It was a world which was quite divorced from humanity but somehow gave him strength and indifference for his job; the job of an official in the Secret Police who had killed more men than he bothered to remember.

As though sensing his thoughts, Radek leaned forward and smiled at Carlin; the small prim smile of a wealthy aunt refusing a loan, the unmarried schoolmaster explaining the facts of life.

"Yes, I am sorry, Mr. Carlin, but, at the same time, if you really haven't got the knowledge, it makes things easier for me. In a moment I must tell you something but first I would like to make my position clear. I would like to show that there is nothing personal in what I may have to do to you.

"You see, like many other people, I have a hobby. In my case it is the study of animals. I like animals very much indeed and human beings merely bore me. It may be a fault in my character but, if I had my way, I would devote my life to that hobby. I would be a game warden, I would sweep out cages in the zoo. I would do anything to be with animals.

"Unfortunately that is impossible for I have a job to

do." He paused and drew back a little. The leatherbound elbows of his shabby suit squeaked slightly on the desk and he might have been confiding his problems to an old and trusted friend.

"Now what is that job, Mr. Carlin? It is not a bad one, though dull. They pay me well and, because I am supposed to bear a certain degree of strain, there are long holidays which make life worth living for me. You will understand that I don't want to lose it.

"There are certain unpleasant duties attached to it however. I have to find things out. I have to find out what a particular person knows and if he is telling me the exact truth. And you are such a person, Mr. Carlin." He broke off and pulled a crumpled packet of cigarettes from the drawer. They were short, dark cigarettes with cardboard mouthpieces. He lit one and watched the first wisps of smoke drift away to the ceiling before he continued.

"Yes, you are a man we hoped would have something to sell us. You came to our country on quite legitimate business and then suddenly we heard you were in a jam. To be exact we received a message from the British police. They stated that you had murdered your wife on the day you left England for the Soviet Union and asked us to send you home to answer that charge. And when I heard about that it seemed there might be a lucky break for both of us.

"So I stopped them sending you home as Scotland Yard asked. You are the director of a firm we have long been interested in so I was nice to you and offered you sanctuary. In return though, I hoped you would give me something; the details of an electrical circuit your company is about to produce.

"But now you tell me that you have no knowledge of this circuit—that you are merely a businessman, not a scientist, and it is only known to your partner, a man called Antoni Marric. For over a week you have said that and at last I am beginning to believe you. Oh, I'm sorry, Mr. Carlin, I have been neglecting my duties as a

8

host." He pushed the cigarettes and lighter across the table.

"And now the time has come for you to realize what is at stake, my friend. The equipment I want deals with the control of guided missiles, does it not? Oh, yes, our agents have been interested in this project for quite some time and have told me a good deal about it. All the same, it is not a vital thing to us; it doesn't matter a great deal to my country, only to me personally. Not worth you risking hell for." Radek broke off and pushed the lighter back in his pocket. For a moment his fingers drummed quietly on the desk.

"Mr. Carlin, do you really believe that this matter is important to history? Do you think that a people who can throw a rocket round the moon need the help of a little tin-pot factory in South London? No, it is not Russia who needs that circuit, but myself. I need it to preserve my job.

"You see the department I work for exists to provide details of military research in the West. By now, it might be thought redundant but it is my job and what I am paid for. If your government adopts this piece of apparatus, which seems possible, I must record it and tell my masters what it consists of and how efficient it is. That is my function in life and my existence depends on it. And, in this case, I will have no excuse for failure, because fortune has thrown you into the hollow of my hand." His hand stopped drumming on the wood and lay open before Peter Carlin. A slim brown hand a woman might have envied; a hand which could be kind in different circumstances.

"But if you really do not have this information, then we must get along without it and no harm will be done. I am employed to find things out, not to work miracles. If you don't have the knowledge I am not asked to invent it. My masters are perhaps ignorant and fanatical men but they won't blame me. They will merely be disappointed and say, 'Poor, old Radek. He did his best but the man knew nothing. Perhaps next time he will be more fortunate.' " He pulled hard on the cigarette for a second and when he put it down he still smiled but the smile was quite different.

"Yes, they will say that, but there is one snag, I'm afraid. I will have to convince them you don't know. I must show you to them and prove that you would have drawn that circuit had you been able. Yes, Mr. Carlin, I will have to demonstrate your ignorance in a very horrible way. Believe me, I don't want to do it, but if it is necessary, I will and with less—far less compunction than I would need to kill a rat.

"So, that's how it is. The circuit in question may not greatly benefit my country or yours and you can either draw it or not. But, if you can, I beg you to do so because I must prove the truth; either way I must prove it.

"And now, Mr. Carlin, are you still sure you can't help me?"

"Yes, I'm sure." Peter Carlin twisted in his chair and looked at the clock on the wall and the calendar below it. Through the sunlight and drifting smoke they seemed vaguely unreal like symbols of a dream. The time was four P.M., the date April 10 and he had been in Leningrad eight days.

"Mr. Carlin," said Radek through the smoke. "Think before you decide. Consider our offer; sanctuary, a house and a state pension for life. Remember that your own country believes you a traitor who has fled to us because of your crime and you will not have one friend to mourn you. Remember that and then, if you can, draw me the circuit for you have nothing to lose."

The clock had spun backwards, the calendar leaves had grown again, the date was April 2, and the time noon. He had nothing to lose except a wife, a partner and the half share of an invention which could make them a fortune.

He was walking down the Nevski Prospekt with a briefcase in his hand and the case contained a conditional contract between the firm of Carlin & Marric and the Soviet Ministry of Rest & Culture. It was a nice thick contract written on parchment and concerned the sale and supply of fifty electric computing machines; net value two hundred and eighty thousand roubles, ten thousand pounds sterling. And that was almost the exact amount they needed to save the firm from the bailiffs.

Oh, yes, at the beginning they'd done well. They'd started with nothing, or nearly nothing, two years after the war. Just three tarred sheds they'd had then, twenty lathes, a battered, out-of-date press and a lot of hope. And sometimes hope paid off. It did if you were prepared to work twenty hours a day every day and your partner was a genius, which was what Toni Marric was.

He, Peter Carlin, had been nothing much. Just the plodder, the work-horse of the team, touring the country in a battered Austin, begging for orders; factory work at first, parts of parts of other peoples' products and near grovelling in his endless search for supplies.

"Just ten tons, sir. If you can only let us have ten tons of steel rod we'll be all right for another month or so. Eight then? Thank you, gentlemen, thank you very much indeed and I won't forget this."

And like Gallio, Toni Marric cared for none of these things. With sublime indifference, he sat in the dusty back room they called the "drawing office" fiddling with bits of wire, scribbling endless calculations on scraps of paper and scowling at the slide-rule as though it were some hostile monster designed to frustrate and defeat him.

Then, sometimes, he would appear. He would come, blinking slightly, into the workshop with a roll of paper in his hand and sidle nervously between the machines.

"Peter," he would say. "Peter, I'm not sure about this, as there's no model yet, but it could just work."

It worked all right. Everything he made worked. The vacuum cleaner was the first. It had twin opposed fans, one blowing, one pulling back and the design was quite new. The men laughed at it at first. "It rips as it tears as

11

it wears," they said, but they were wrong. It did exactly what he thought it would, removing the dust without touching the carpet pile and it was ahead of everything else on the market.

And the cleaner was only the beginning. After it the patents came out like an oil gush and every one was just a little in front of its nearest competitor.

Their rivals copied them, of course, they had to. They took Toni Marric's ideas and they prettied them up with chrome and paint and plastic and, whenever it was possible, they cut the price. They copied him all they could but they couldn't copy his mind. And one day Peter Carlin, the plodder, the salesman, the work-horse, looked through the accounts and knew they had built a business. It was on that day he first met Susan Rayne.

He had sat in the restaurant looking idly at the door and feeling pleased with the firm's progress and secure for the first time in years. Then the door had opened, Susan had come in and, at the mere sight of her, he knew she was what he wanted, what he had to have.

Not that there was anything very striking about her on the surface. Her features were good but not really beautiful. Her figure and clothes were good too but there was nothing showy about them. Yet, as she stood there, looking round for a table, every man in that crowded room seemed to stare at her; for she had time behind her.

You take a field and you level it and drain it and cover it with turf. Then, through the years, you roll and sweep and manure it and every summer week you cut the grass. You look for weeds as though they were plague spots and, whenever there's a dry spell, you water it. You go on doing that for a hundred years and at last, if you've been lucky and the soil's good, you have a lawn; a lawn which will make the mower advertisements look like stubble fields.

And Susan Rayne was like that lawn, for there were twenty generations of money and breeding behind her. Eight hundred years with nothing to do but balance the line of the neck, the pride of the eye and the poise of mind and body. To Peter Carlin, doctor's son from the Midlands, self-made businessman, admirer of symmetry, she was the top, the last complete design; the unobtainable which had to be obtained.

And somehow he did obtain it. There was the sudden rain storm, the shared taxi, a discovery of mutual interests and reserve breaking down into laughter. There was dancing at the intimate clubs, a visit to the factory and a long car racing to the coast. And at last he'd sat before a polished table with a glass of brandy before him and watched an old man smile at the end of a dark, candle-lit room.

He'd heard of Walter Rayne of course, seen pictures of him, but the reality was far more impressive. A tall, old man who held himself very straight to hide his age and the crooked spine a hunting field had given him so many years ago. A man who was two men; the aristocrat who lived alone with a retinue of almost feudal retainers and the man who wanted to pay back a little of what his ancestors had taken. Cancer research, prisoners' aid, moral welfare, old peoples' homes; there was hardly a charity in Britain which did not owe something to Sir Walter Rayne. And now the two people in him were fighting a battle over Peter Carlin.

"And so you are going to marry my daughter," he said from the end of that long, long room. "Very well, I suppose I must give my blessing. Susan is of age and knows her own mind." His voice was gentle and low but somehow commanding; an instrument polished and tuned through centuries.

"All the same, this marriage worries me a little, Mr. Carlin. There is so much time between us, you know. I say that with no disparagement at all, just as a fact which exists. You see our family is old and yours is young. Our vitality is almost burned out while yours is just beginning. We are rather like those characters in a Matthew Arnold poem—'The tired Tyrian trader and the young, light-hearted master of the wave.'

"Yes, there are many things about us you will not be

13

able to understand and we will find some of your ways strange too. And Susan herself is a strange girl. Her mother died when she was very young and I have not been a good father. I spent too much time holding this estate together and running various other projects, to give my daughter what she needed.

"No, as a child, Susan spent most of her time wandering alone in this house and grounds and she must have been very lonely—lonely and perhaps afraid." He looked up for a moment and, in the candle light, it seemed as if only the eyes were holding his face together.

"Yes, as I say, I give you my blessing but please try and do something for me in return. There may come a day when you find Susan strange and possibly difficult. Pardon that and try to make her happy. Yes, make her happy and give her some of the love I was unable to give."

And, at the beginning, there had been no need for that plea of warning because they were happy; they were terribly happy. Even sitting as he did now, in the building of the Russian Secret Police, Peter could remember with pleasure how happy they'd been.

Yes, in the window behind Radek's desk, he could see the image of Susan's face. He could see the way her nose wrinkled slightly when she smiled and how she laughed that night when they walked home from the opera and how her hair blew loose as the Bentley purred through the great streets of Europe; Kaiserdamm, Victor Hugo, Primo Rivera.

Yes, they'd been happy, though not as a secure married couple, but as lovers. Only as lovers, for though their bodies clung together there was always something between them. Something in Susan which shut him out and which he could never share. And, at last that thing stepped into the light and there came the time and day that Walter Rayne had spoken of.

It came suddenly, for she was just there one moment and then not there. He kissed her good-bye in the morning when he left for the factory and when he returned home she had gone away and there was a woman he didn't know waiting for him.

It was as if something had happened to Susan and it was something too bad to talk about or even cry about. There was suddenly no contact at all between him and that woman with her set, haunted face who would never speak of the thing which troubled her. The girl he married had died and he was left with somebody who was locked behind a gauze curtain so he could never see what she was thinking. A woman who spent her days wandering without apparent aim round the city and her nights lying awake on the spare bed or writing in a diary he was never allowed to look at.

He tried to talk, of course; to help her fight the thing that haunted and had changed her but it was useless and there seemed no way round the barrier which separated them. She wouldn't or couldn't tell him anything, and when he pressed it always ended in the same way, dumb refusal, the head thrown back and footsteps walking quickly out of the room.

And he tried doctors too, but she refused to see them, and, on the surface, looked physically well. At the end, he tried her father.

He wouldn't forget that day. He'd only seen Walt Rayne three times before and always in the shadows of his dark library. Standing in the flat he looked just the same, tall and straight and impressive, but somehow out of place; a very old building lit up by overbright flood lamps. He hadn't removed his coat or even sat down, but just stood there listening to Peter. Then he turned and walked through to Susan's bedroom alone.

It couldn't have been half an hour before he came out of that room, but it might have been a hundred years. For, when Rayne pulled the door behind him, he wasn't impressive any more and he certainly wasn't straight. He was just an old, bent man shuffling across the carpet who was tired—terribly tired. And beneath the tired lines of his face there was a great bitterness. He was like a stag that has run too long before the hounds and knows the end of the chase is in sight.

"I'm sorry," he said in a voice that was no longer a tuned instrument but cracked and broken. "I really am sorry, my boy, but, as I told you, Susan has always been a strange girl." He tightened his coat and, without another word, turned and walked through to the lift and his waiting car.

Peter began to give up after that. He still prayed that one day a change might come and she would tell him what troubled her but he resigned himself to his life. And suddenly his work became more vital than ever, for the factory was beginning to fail.

It was partly his own fault of course. During the early years of struggle and scraping he had nursed the business like a mother and ruled Toni Marric with a hand of iron. For, though possibly a genius, Toni was half Italian, half Irish with the impetuosity of both races and he cared little for profit and loss. The fun of invention was his life and it was Peter Carlin, the man of business, who had to encourage this scheme because it might pay and discard another as impracticable. But, since his marriage, Peter had taken less and less active interest in the firm and, on his own, Toni Marric had become a crusader.

"No more rubbish, Pete," he said standing beside his table with a light in his face that had not been there before. "No more gadgets, no more cleaners or hair dryers. This is what I have to do, what I must do, what I am going to do and I don't give a damn if I break the business doing it."

And he nearly had broken the business. Peter looked through the accounts and saw the red figures piling up and the orders unfulfilled and the supplies unpaid-for and the hands standing idle round the machines because they were without work or direction. Then he went up to Toni's dusty drawing office and looked at the big diagram pinned to the wall.

"All right, old man," he said. "Maybe we'll make it, but tell me about it first. Be as simple as you can though, because I'm no technician."

He listened quietly while Toni explained and, though half the details made no sense at all, he soon saw what the thing was to become.

You build a rocket and you put a motor or propellant in it that will take it the distance you want and you let it loose. You have instruments inside to control it against pressure and wind force and the pull of gravity and, if those instruments are working correctly, it should end up right in the centre of the target.

It doesn't though. Always—almost always it is miles off course because you just don't know the shape of the earth. You know that it's not flat but like an orange punched in at the ends but that's about all you do know. You can't tell how the mass of one mountain range will draw your rocket towards it or a flat plane deflect its course. You don't know enough about your own planet to tell that.

But Toni Marric hoped to know. If his calculations were correct, the machine he planned would tell him those facts. It would send out rays from the nose of the rocket and the rays would bounce back to cancel the mountain's pull and the lowland's thrust and death would go home, just where they wanted it.

And, after a time, Peter Carlin saw they had to go on with it. He had lost his hold on Toni now and the machine had to be built. They took the drawings to a tall building in London where a very smart gentleman in a frock coat and a carnation in his button-hole talked to them, and then showed them into another room where the men who mattered were waiting.

And the men who mattered weren't smart and they hardly spoke at all. There were two of them in ill-fitting suits and glasses and they were like children with a new toy as they examined the drawings. There was an American officer in a suspiciously quiet uniform there too but

17

he seemed to play no part in the proceedings. He just stood and listened and, once or twice, made notes in a leatherbound pocket book.

But they weren't really interested, not yet. They liked the idea, they felt it might work but they wanted completion before they talked business. And, to complete, the firm would need ten thousand pounds. Ten thousand to fill a box with two yards of wire, a pound of lead, a little glass, crystal and polythene; the means to send a rocket home.

So Peter went out to get that ten thousand pounds. The Anglo-Russian trade agreement was in force, the Russians said they needed office equipment and the firm's computing machine was as good as anything in its price range. He got his visa, packed the specifications in a brief-case and took a plane to Leningrad with his sales-patter in his head.

"Well, this is it, gentlemen. To be quite frank it doesn't have all the refinements of the Hollerith machine—not quite as impressive looking either. All the same it does its job, takes far less room and costs rather less money." A slight pause for a smile there and the final cliché. "And that, you must agree, is an important point, gentlemen."

But he didn't see any "gentlemen." He saw a pleasant, middle-aged woman at the Ministry of Culture who gave him tea and talked about life in England and the Soviet Union and hoped he would have an enjoyable stay.

And she was an easy person to do business with. She quite saw how, with the new trade agreement, he had wanted to get to Russia before his rivals and had had no time to book an air passage for a sample machine. She would have to look at one of course but the specifications seemed quite satisfactory and she would be glad to sign a provisional agreement.

Then she took out two sheets of creamy parchment paper and signed at the foot of them. And Peter Carlin signed too. He signed with a cheerful, sweeping flourish for the contract would go through and they would have the money to build Toni's circuit and save the firm. He felt a slight shadow of guilt as he thought about that, because the circuit might well be the means of destroying that pleasant woman and the city she lived in.

And finally he finished his tea and shook hands with her and went out. He dismissed the car they had put at his disposal and started to walk back to his hotel. He preferred to walk because the long winter was breaking into spring and the air felt gay and exciting and the contract in his case gave him the right to stop being a businessman and play tourist for a while.

There was only one cloud in his sky and it was so far away. As he had packed in London two nights before, Susan had lain on the bed watching him. She hadn't spoken a word but somehow he knew she wanted him to stay. For the first time in months she wanted him with her and, if he had stayed, she might have told him the thing that troubled her.

He hadn't stayed though. The firm needed money, the plane left at midnight and he had to find ten thousand pounds; ten thousand to fill a metal box with common materials. Net value one pound seven shillings and sixpence. He had picked up his case and walked out to the waiting car.

But, after all, that cloud might be a good omen. Perhaps the very appeal in her eyes showed the start of a new beginning. He'd be home tomorrow and then possibly— just possibly he'd find the stranger had left the flat and the woman he married was home again. He glanced at his watch and walked briskly down the street, watching the little grey-green buses and the sun playing on the city that Czars had built. He had exactly an hour before lunch and, with that time to kill, turned left towards the Neva Bridge.

And he never reached it. In front of him was the loom of Peter and Paul Fortress and he heard a tug bellow three times on the river. He paused for a moment to light a cigarette, striking a match on the parapet. It was at that moment he felt the hand on his shoulder.

The clock had turned forward, the calendar leaves had blown away, the time was 4 P.M., the date April 10, and Radek no longer smiled.

Radek had stopped smiling and he stood by the window with a buff folder in his hand. He turned the pages slowly as though they were too heavy for him and his voice was low and bored as though repeating a dull lesson to a backward child.

"Before you make your final decision, Mr. Carlin, I think it only fair I go through the facts with you once more. As I said before, you must realize there is nothing to hope for from your own country. In their eyes, you are already a murderer and a traitor. In fact you are dead and buried." He glanced once more at the folder and then opened his hand. As it dropped, the pages came loose from the binding and fluttered to the floor like autumn leaves.

"You came to the Soviet Union, Mr. Carlin, in the hope of signing a routine business agreement between your company and one of our ministries. I hear your mission was successful but that doesn't concern me at all.

"What concerns me is this. After you had been in Russia a very short time, we received a communication from Scotland Yard. It seems they wanted our help. They asked us to send you home on the first available plane so you could answer a certain charge—the charge of murdering your wife."

There was a bust of Khrushchev on Radek's desk and, as he spoke, it seemed to smile at Peter; the fat friendly smile of a plaster pirate; a Toby jug.

"Well, our police arrested you but, before putting you on the plane, they asked Scotland Yard for a full transcript of the case against you, there being no extradition agreement between our two countries. When this was received they had the good sense to communicate with my department. For some time I have been interested in the activities of your firm and I felt we should have a little chat.

"And we had it, didn't we? I told you what we knew and you gave your side of the story. You told me that you knew nothing of your wife's death and, I must say, you seemed upset about it. You stated that, for some time, she had been in an odd state of mind and seemed to be hiding something. You said that, on the night you left for Russia, you went out of your flat about nine o'clock and drove to your factory as you wanted to go through certain papers before making the trip. You were a little over an hour there but the night watchman on duty never saw you. Yes, I know he is an old and possibly idle man but it seems odd that he never saw you or heard your car.

"And, when you had been through the papers you wanted, you say you drove straight to Gatwick Airport which is about thirty miles away. You left your car in the public park there and took the midnight plane to Leningrad. That is your story, Mr. Carlin, but now let's see what the police say. No, please do not interrupt me." He held up his hand and might have been a schoolmaster before and unruly class.

"The police agree that you left the flat at about nine but they say you weren't alone. Your wife went with you. They were very frank with us when we asked for a transcript and let us have a full report of the evidence.

"Your wife's maid, Ethel Sommers, who had been with the Rayne family all her life and should be a reliable witness, made a statement it seems. She told the police that during the evening you and your wife had a violent quarrel. This passed however and at about eight-thirty you seemed on the best of terms. Mrs. Carlin told the maid she was going down to see you off at the airport and would stay the night at the Reigate cottage you owned. Ethel Sommers packed an overnight bag for her mistress and saw you drive off together just after nine.

"Well, in the morning, Miss Sommers rang up your wife at Reigate. She wanted to speak to her about some routine domestic matter but, when there was no reply, she became worried. At about noon, she contacted the police.

"And your car wasn't parked at the airport, my friend. It was outside the door of that cottage with a woman's case on the back seat and your fingerprints and only yours on the wheel and the gear-shift. And on the front passenger seat they found blood, a great deal of blood; your wife's blood, Mr. Carlin. Ah, will you excuse me one minute, please."

There was a fluttering of wings against the glass behind him and Radek turned and took a tin from the desk. Then he opened the window and all at once he looked quite different, alive and excited and not bored at all.

And the thrush was obviously a regular visitor. She stood quite calmly on the sill and allowed his fingers to run up and down over the plumage of her head and neck while Radek tilted the tin and dropped three worms before her.

"Well, Luba, my lovely girl," he said. "You're late, aren't you? Half past three is your regular time and it's well after four now. I was beginning to get worried about you." He watched the bird start to gulp down the worms and then grinned at Peter Carlin.

"She has been coming every day for three weeks now. I think she must be nesting somewhere nearby which is rare in the centre of the city. I always give her three and she eats two and carries one home with her. See, she is off now." He gave the bird a final pat as it picked up the remaining worm and flew off in the direction of the river.

"Yes, for three weeks she has been coming to see me and always about the same time. And talking of time, Mr. Carlin, I think ours has almost run out now."

He replaced the tin and pressed the switch of a big, old-fashioned intercom. His Russian was very quick as he spoke into it and carried a marked accent of Besarabia, but Peter could just catch the words. "You may send our friends up now. Tell them to wait outside."

"And now, let's go on with your story, shall we? When the police saw that blood, they broke into the cottage.

22

They had to break in because it was locked and they never found the key. We did though. We found it here in Leningrad when we searched your bag." He reached in his pocket and threw something on the desk. The little brass Yale key glinted like gold against the stained wood.

"And inside the cottage they found your wife. She was lying under the bed and she had been shot through the back of the neck at close range. The bullet had passed out through her lower jaw and was never found.

"The gun was, though. A thirty-two Enfield revolver, fired once and your prints and yours alone were on it. It was in the pocket of the car where it had every right to be because you have a permit to carry it. In the past you were in the habit of taking large sums of money between the bank and your works and that gun was quite legitimate protection. That is the police evidence against you, Mr. Carlin."

And, all the time, as he had repeated the evidence, Radek had studied the man before him. A tall, dark man sitting listlessly in the clamped chair and the man's eyes were just tired and full of bewilderment. A man who didn't look like a killer, but then, who did? Gregor Radek had little faith in appearances, and none in human nature and he saw how it might have been.

He pictured the row between husband and wife patched up, and the woman's offer to accompany her husband to the airport, and the little gun tucked away in the glove compartment. Then, in the car, the quarrel had blazed out again, there had been the sudden flash of anger, the means of death, ready and waiting at hand's reach, and the bullet had gone home.

If that were the truth, the rest was easy to follow. The cottage was nearby and presented a hiding place. Carlin had a passport and a ticket to Russia in his pocket. The plane left at midnight. If he panicked that plane would have seemed a temporary solution; a way out for a frightened and no longer quite sane man.

But Radek wasn't really convinced, for Peter Carlin didn't look as if he'd panic. He looked cool and efficient and intelligent. Far too intelligent to commit a stupid bungling crime like this and try to run from it. No, it was quite possible he was telling the exact truth and had been framed.

And that had nothing to do with Radek. Radek's job was quite clear. He had to suppose him guilty. He had to convince this man that his case was hopeless and he had nothing to lose. He had to break his mind and his will and persuade him to talk. To talk about a little, rather unimportant circuit that the department was paid to know about.

"And I wonder why you didn't take the car with you," he said. "Did the blood on the seat horrify you or was it for a rather more practical reason? Did you think that if the car was left outside the cottage it might be supposed your wife had driven it back from the airport and been killed, by some vagrant perhaps, much later on?

"In any event, you left the car and walked to Reigate station. There is a train from there which reaches Gatwick at eleven-thirty. I think you took that train and then joined the midnight plane for Russia. I think that is the whole story.

"And now, now, Mr. Carlin, let's stop beating about the bush. Do you still ask me to believe you didn't kill your wife?"

"No, I don't ask you to believe anything," Peter pulled hard on the cigarette and closed his eyes. He didn't care about Radek any more, or what Radek said, or what Radek might do to him. He just wanted to think. To think about Susan and the person who killed her.

For somebody had killed her. Somebody had killed her in a car he knew was parked at the airport. Somebody had blasted her face with a gun, they said, that bore his prints. Somebody who had planned well and carefully to make him seem a fugitive and a murderer. Somebody who could persuade a very loyal, very honest and rather simple-minded servant to tell a deliberate and complicated lie. Somebody who must have known his exact movements.

24

Nothing made sense to him any more, nothing fitted or held together but, as he sat in the room waiting for Radek to finish with him, he had strangely no fear at all but just one big, pulsing, hating desire, to see the face of the person who killed his wife.

And Susan must have known that that person was coming. She had looked at him while he packed and her eyes had asked him to stay. After all those months of separation she had wanted that, because she must have known that when he left, somebody was coming to call for her.

He thought of her during those past months and how she had wandered the city by day, and at night sat writing in a diary he was never allowed to look at. Perhaps in that diary was the name of the one who had killed her.

But he hadn't stayed. The firm needed ten thousand pounds, the Leningrad plane left at midnight and he had gone out. He had gone and left her with Ethel Sommers and driven round via the factory, taking two and a half hours for a forty-minute journey. And, because of that, Susan was dead and he was sitting before a man who loved animals and cared nothing for humanity. A man who didn't even care for Russia very much but merely wanted to preserve his job; the job of an official in the Secret Service.

"Well, it doesn't really matter, Mr. Carlin," said Radek very quietly. "I don't care if you are a murderer or not. All that concerns me is that you are a partner in a firm which is trying to produce a certain piece of equipment I am paid to know about. A piece of equipment I am prepared to buy from you. And to buy at a good price.

"So, sell it to me, my friend, because you have nothing to lose. When we refused to send you home your people would naturally think you had gone over to us and turned traitor to save your skin. They will believe you have already given us that circuit and, apart from myself, you are without a friend in the world."

There was a slight change in Radek's expression as he said that and, for a moment, it seemed to Peter that he really was a friend. That he honestly did want to help him.

"Yes, I can be a good friend to you. I will not only give you sanctuary but a comfortable life as well; a villa on the Neva and a state pension. You will not be an outcast here, but an honoured guest of my country.

"So there are just two alternatives before you. Either you draw me the circuit or I shall ring a bell and the door will open. There are people waiting behind that door at this moment. They are not pleasant people, but they are experts. They know the ways to truth—the way to break a man." He turned from the window and rested his hand on a bell-push by the desk. He didn't press it but his fingers ran across the button as though touching a rare and beautiful object.

"And now, Mr. Carlin, for the last time, will you give me your answer?"

And Peter Carlin gave it. He was an accused murderer, a supposed traitor and somebody had killed his wife and framed him for it. He was sitting before a Russian intelligence officer and he knew quite well what would happen to him. But he gave his answer. He had to because he just didn't care any more. Susan was dead and soon he would be dying but he didn't care. He was just tired of it. He was tired of the "Yard" report and tired of Radek and Radek's old-maid smile and Radek's animal pictures on the wall. He was sick and tired of them.

He thought of words but, all at once, he knew they were no more use to him and he didn't need words. He looked at the desk and saw what his answer had to be. He leaned forward and ground his cigarette into the bronze eye of Khrushchev's bust.

And Radek's expression didn't alter. He raised his eyebrows slightly, but he still looked prim and bored and indifferent.

"Thank you," he said. "A very nice clear reply which saves me further work.

"Yes, I have finished with you now, Mr. Carlin, and I don't expect we shall meet again. Now, I have to give you to the experts—to the people who always find the ways to truth." He leaned forward, pulled out a handkerchief and began to wipe the ash from the bust. When he went on he might have been speaking to himself.

"There are so many ways to truth, you know, so many ways of crushing a human spirit. If one is modern there are drugs and hypnosis. If one has a historical background you can copy the methods of the Inquisition. Put a man in a glass room for instance, a room of mirrors, and leave him alone with himself. In time he becomes so disgusted with what he sees that he will crack.

"But all those complicated methods take time and my masters are impatient men who have given me no time at all. I have had to order something quicker for you." The bronze head was quite clean now and he folded the handkerchief and tucked it back in his pocket.

"And, all the same, I'm sorry for you, Mr. Carlin. You may, or may not know the circuit, but either way, I'm sorry. I believe you have a saying in England which goes —'*out of the frying-pan into the fire.*' Well, you've finished with the pan at last and the time has come to meet the fire."

He sat down and pressed the bell. The door opened and the people who knew the ways to truth came into the room.

There were three men and two of them were without importance. They were short and thick-set and wore tight, dark suits and their faces were the flat, expressionless masks of the Tartar. They came into the room and they stood behind Peter's chair and they smelled. They smelled of wind and weather and horses and the strong, acid sweat of primitive men. They didn't matter in the slightest.

And the man who followed them did not smell. To sweat would have been too natural a function for him. He closed the door and, for a moment, he leaned against it watching Peter Carlin. Then, very slowly, he began to walk forward.

And he was such an ordinary man. He was medium sized, medium coloured and middle-aged. There was a hint of a scar below his receding hair-line and his dark blue tie clashed slightly with the pale blue of his eyes, but there was nothing remarkable about him. An ordinary man you might find in any office, any factory or shop, anywhere in the world. His mouth was the worst thing Peter had seen on a human face.

The man came across the room and there was something odd about his walk. The feet moved as though on puppet strings without direction from his mind and his body seemed slack and lifeless as he stopped before the chair and looked down at Peter Carlin. Looked down at him with very pale, blue eyes; pale, china blue eyes; eyes which had something wrong with them.

"We took many things from Germany after the war," said Radek behind the desk. "We took machines and raw materials and gold. We took people as well sometimes; scientists and engineers, doctors and technicians. And one of those technicians was called Rudi Klee. Can you guess his technique, Mr. Carlin? Do I need tell you what he is?"

And there was no need. He could see from the pale eyes, the walk, the hang of the body and the shape of that terrible mouth. This man might once have been a human being but he had been turned into a machine; a machine which had been designed and built and tuned for just one purpose—to perform one task and to solve a single problem—the problem of pain.

And they said they'd got them all. They'd shouted it on the radio and blazoned it in the press. They said they'd shot them, hanged them, destroyed them utterly; those dark people from the places whose names still conjured up terror—Belsen and Buchenwald, Auschwitz and Sachsenhausen; Josef Kramer, Irma Graese, Otto Lang.

But the press and the radio had lied because they weren't all dead and one of them was standing before him now. He was standing quite still with his blue eyes watching Peter and hands were pulling Peter up towards him.

And, just before Peter reached his full height, the man moved. He moved sideways, as though falling, and, at the same instant his right shoe drew back. It was a very respectable, well-polished shoe of about size nine, but its tip wasn't polished at all for it was steel. It drew back, hung there for an instant, and then came forward quickly.

Peter screamed. He screamed like a child and it wasn't from the shock or the pain in his groin where the steel point went home. Pain was fire and ice turning to choking nausea but it wasn't just pain that made him cry out and fight madly against the hands which were dragging him to the door. He screamed because, just as the man kicked him, he seemed to look right through his eyes and see the thing that made the mouth the shape it was.

"Radek," he said. "Radek, you can't, you can't do it. I don't know the circuit, I swear that I never knew it. So please, Radek." And finally—"For the love of God, Radek!"

But Radek didn't believe in God and he was no longer there. He had done the job he was paid to do and was taking a well-deserved break. He never heard Peter Carlin cry out or even glanced at the struggling figures in the doorway—he was far too busy.

He was sitting at his desk drawing something on a pad. There was a look of great love and pleasure on his face as he sat there drawing. And, when he had finished, the picture showed the head of a dormouse.

CHAPTER TWO

THE black Tchaika saloon resembled a Packard, but Detroit wouldn't have owned her. Detroit would have turned up its nose at the heavy, out-of-date suspension, the hobledehoy coachwork and the big engine that produced half a Packard's power. She was like an American car in everything except American know-how and craftsmanship.

Yet, for all her failings, the Tchaika had one interesting feature unknown to the engineers of Detroit. At either end of her wide rear seat there were two steel rings. Peter Carlin was chained to them.

Peter half sat, half lay back against the rexine covers with his arms outstretched as the handcuffs held them and he tried not to think at all. He didn't look at the man who sat before him on the bucket seat behind the driver but the man's atmosphere was all around him in the car as strong as a gas turning to a solid. He forced his mind away from that man and the future he held for him but, all the time, thought imposed itself.

The man was taking him out to a quiet house in the country where they could be alone together and talk about truth. The man knew a great deal about truth for these were an efficient and economical people who employed experts.

Yes, they'd been efficient. Somehow they had heard of the thing the factory was trying to produce and, when they knew about Susan's murder, they'd acted. They'd been so nice at first too; taking him into their hearts and bribing him. "There is no need for you to go home and face trial, Mr. Carlin," they'd said. "Play it smart now. You help us and we'll look after you."

Oh, yes, they'd been nice; the offer of safety, a state pension and a house by the river. He wondered what he would have done if he'd really been a murderer, had really known the facts they wanted. But it was no good thinking about that for he had not killed Susan and he had nothing to sell them. Only Toni Marric had that knowledge. And, all the time, while they made their offers, the quiet men in bars and trains and airports had spread the word and his own country knew him for a traitor.

And slowly they had become sure that he couldn't help them, that he was useless to them, but it wasn't enough. For, to preserve his job, Radek needed not sureness, but certainty.

So now, he lay back in a big car with a rug across his body to hide his chained hands and an ex-concentration camp guard sat in front of him.

For a moment like a child cheating at prayers, his eyes flicked over the man before him. He took in the calmness of the man and the ordinariness of him and the complete lack of expression on his face. The face of the unloved and the unloving with just one skill, one talent at his command. The face which would take him apart and find what he knew and did not know, what he could stand and what was unendurable to him.

They were out of the city now and running north. It had to be north because they had crossed the bridge; the same bridge where he had first been arrested. Grey, Czarist stone gave way to Soviet concrete, the bus-stops ended and the last allotments fell back before clumps of pine and birch.

And then there were more houses which he recognized from picture postcards. The houses of Pushkin Village, still preserved as a monument, with the red flag above the door where another Peter had stood; Peter the Great, Czar of all the Russians, watching the building of the city that once took his name. The car passed quickly through that village and then there were no more houses

31

at all. Just flat, dull country broken by an occasional ditch and clumps of silver birch.

The road was wooden now. Even in his despair, Peter Carlin noticed that. It rested on piles driven deep into the soft earth with cross pieces between them and thick boards above the crosses—the road of a country where timber and labour were cheap. The wheels clicked sharply on the boards and, through the mirror, he could see the driver's face as he concentrated to hold the car at speed.

And he knew the driver. It was the same man who had met him at the airport and taken him to his hotel and then to the Ministry. It was strange, that, and seemed to confirm the efficiency of these people. They had been watching him from the moment he arrived in Russia.

The driver's name was Ilya—yes, that was right, Ilya Malendin. He was a pleasant man and seemed friendly. Peter had sat in the front seat and they had talked together as though they were friends.

They had talked about Ilya's family, a wife and three small children which he adored. They had discussed football and the respective costs of living in England and the Soviet Union. Ilya had even spoken of his job as a Ministry driver; the advantages in money and housing it carried and his constant dread of losing it.

Yes, he had a real fear of that, for he felt he was sick. It was nothing serious, he said. Just the odd, stabbing pain when he was tired, but, if they found anything at his next medical examination, he would lose that pleasant well-paid job, his comfortable flat and the hope of a pension.

Peter watched the kindly, anxious face in the mirror and, for part of a second, hope came.

For could it just be that Ilya Malendin was the way out, his salvation? Was Ilya the character in the story books who was going to save him? Was he the miracle worker, the Scarlet Pimpernel, The Western Agent who had watched over him all the time and would shortly reveal himself? The quick blow with the spanner at Rudi Klee's head, the foot hard down on the accelerator and the big car racing for Finland. It was only a small hope though and soon it died.

For there was no hope for him now and no miracle. Ilya was just a man who drove a car and would do exactly what his masters told him. They were travelling north along a deserted road to a quiet house where he would meet pain and nothing could prevent that meeting. In front of him, he saw the man on the bucket seat smile as though in remembrance of pleasures often tasted but never fulfilled and he closed his eyes.

He closed his eyes tightly, leaning back as the chains made him, and he gave up hope. There was no room for hope any more. Nobody would come to his aid and no miracle would save him. He would never know who killed Susan. All he would know was terror and pain from the man before him so he closed his eyes tightly, as though hiding beneath a blanket.

And it was a pity he did that because, just as he closed them, the miracle happened and he never saw it. Ilya Malendin died.

The human heart is a pump made of muscle and membrane and it has two compression chambers controlled by two valves. Every thirty seconds, at six fluid ounces per second, it forces blood around the body and, under normal conditions, it will go on doing that till age withers it.

But Ilya Malendin's condition was not normal. Over the years sclerosis had furred up his arteries, the pipes that lead from the heart, and every time those chambers compressed, sixty-eight times a minute, sixty minutes an hour, twenty-four hours a day, the valves clotted up a little more and didn't open quite so freely. And, at last, one of them didn't open at all and he died.

He got no warning. One moment he was holding the wheel and concentrating on the road and the next he was holding nothing at all. His hands were suddenly just weights at the end of his arms, his foot wouldn't move to the brake and he felt a steel spike coming out through the centre of his chest. And that was the last thing he ever did feel, for he was dead.

The Tchaika weighed over two tons and it was traveling at sixty miles an hour. The crankshaft of her eight-cylinder engine revolved three thousand three hundred times a minute and it kept on revolving because a dead man's foot was pressed on the throttle. She came straight down the road, ignoring a bend, and hit the parapet. For an instant, her wheels seemed to hang against it, then she rose in a bouncing arc towards a clump of trees.

It must have been about four minutes when Peter came round. It couldn't have been much more because the off-side front wheel was still turning and it couldn't have been less because the birds had started to sing again.

The birds were singing, the sun was shining and he was alive. He looked around him at the ruin of the car and the things in it and then, very slowly, he raised his right arm and found it was free, for the chain had torn away from the bolt that held it. There was a terrible pain in his shoulders where the hooks had held him back but he could still use his hand. He looked at it, flexing the muscles and watching the fingers move, then he raised it and pushed back the body of the man who had saved his life.

For though Rudi Klee had been the worst person he had ever known, his death had saved him. He had died when the car hit the first tree and the steering column had burst backwards like a lance to spear him through the partition. And his body had been a shield for Peter Carlin against the column and the engine and the flying glass and the debris that had swept towards him.

For a long time he looked at the stuff that had once been a man and then leaned forward and forced his hand to reach for a pocket. The key to the chains was warm and wet but it gleamed like silver as he drew it out.

Perhaps five minutes Peter remained in that ruin of a car and, when he had found everything that could help him, he crawled out through the broken door to the ground. The earth was soft and cool and smelled of the promise of spring. He lay down on it for a while, nursing his strained shoulder and fighting the desire to vomit. He also tried to give a little thanks to whatever power had saved him so far. Then he got up and started to walk into the woods.

About three hundred yards from the road there was a pool of brackish water and in it he washed his body and removed the worst stains from his clothes. While he waited for them to dry he sat down and counted his assets.

They weren't many and the debits far outnumbered them. The countryside seemed deserted but some time they had to find the car. And, when it was found, the word would go back to Radek and the hunt would be up.

And, even if the miracle continued, and he got out of Russia, would there be any hope for him? In the eyes of the West, he was not only a killer but a traitor too; the man who had done the unforgivable; the pariah who was fit for nothing except death. No, he could expect no help or mercy from his own people.

On his side, he had a body which was free from chains and miraculously unbroken. He had Rudi Klee's passport which bore the seal of the Secret Police and Klee's face was so ordinary, so lacking in expression, that they might accept the picture as his own. He spoke good German and a little Russian and he had two hundred roubles in notes —mainly twenties and mainly new. He was glad they were twenties for the scarlet didn't clash with the stains on their borders. He had these few things—his tools against the world.

And there was one other thing on his side which could not be counted in material terms but would help more than all the rest. It was hatred. Before the smash, he had lost hope but, now he was free, hope no longer mattered. He had no need for hope any more and no fear for himself; only hatred. Hate for the person who had killed his wife and doomed him to rot in Russia. Hatred and the will for revenge were great, shining lamps before him as he sat by the pool and waited for his clothes to dry.

And, when they were dry, he put them on and started to walk back to the town. It would be a long walk and there would be a long journey beyond it. Every man's hand would be against him and his only assets were language, a special passport, a little money and rage. Rage held him up and guided his steps and it was a purely primitive creature, bent on revenge, who walked through the pine woods.

Yes, he had a long way to go; all the way across Europe and every mile would hold an enemy. A long, lonely road with no friend to guide him and he had not even a definite idea of what he was looking for. All the same, if he finished that journey, if he got home and reached a certain spot on the map, he might just find what he wanted —the person, persons or thing that had killed his wife.

And, a thousand miles away, the person who had killed Susan sat at a table and smiled. There was a newspaper spread out on the table and a telephone rest beside it. The voice on the phone was soft and gentle but it sounded odd; it purred. The contented purr of a cat who knows the mouse is exactly where it should be.

"Yes, of course, I have seen the papers," said the voice, "and I rather think we can relax at last. Mr. Carlin has been publicly branded as a traitor and the matter is finished. Yes, that is quite correct. We have buried him alive."

For a long time the voice went on speaking and then slowly the phone was lowered into its rest. The hand that held it was rather like the voice. A nice, well-kept hand, but odd. It was without scar or blemish but still deformed. The fingers were as broad as a man's but as short as a child's. They had only one joint and the nails grew where the knuckles should have been.

CHAPTER THREE

THE southern winds come without warning to the divided city. One day it is still winter, with a grey sky over the broken Victory Arch, the ground hard round the Wannsee lakes and you walk quickly and shiver a little in the shadow of the ruins.

And, all at once, it changes. The winds run up the long roads from the south and west, the earth softens and, overnight, the trees start to put on leaves. Then you still walk fast, but for a different reason, and you smile at the grass breaking through the rubble and look up at the pale and very clear sky; the pale mitteleuropäische sky that breeds songs and folk-tales and sometimes monsters.

It was at that season of the year when Peter Carlin came to Berlin.

He stood at the end of a platform on the Friederichstrasse Station and he felt more naked than the day he was born. Above his head, loud-speakers blared martial music, to his right a locomotive ticked like a gigantic clock and, in front of him, his fellow passengers hurried to the barriers.

And every one of those passengers looked strangely furtive. They had no need to be because probably all of them would be on official business but they still seemed worried. For this was the end of the line, the final check point, the gateway to the West.

And, up to now, it had all been easy for him. He remembered the lucky hitch-hike to Leningrad, the clerk giving him his ticket from the booth and the way the policeman at the gate had glanced at his passport; such a respectful glance when he saw the stamp on its cover and he had not even bothered to open it. Peter had blessed the power of the Secret Police at that moment.

At the frontiers it had been just the same too. At the Polish they had not disturbed him and, at the German, there had been the same quick glance, a salute and the respectful hand giving it back to him.

Yes, these were an economical people; they didn't check because they had no need. This was all their country, their sphere of influence, their prison.

But here, at Berlin, he knew it would be quite different. Here, not actually at the station but only a mile further west, was the rent in the imagined curtain, the bent bar in the cage, the gap in the wall, the way out. Here they would start to be careful. He looked around him at the wire mesh separating the platform from the booking hall and, picking up his newly bought case, started to walk towards the barrier.

The guards on the gate were very young, almost boys, but they looked hard and efficient. They had machine pistols slung over their blue "Volkspolizei" uniforms and a black Alsatian dog crouched beside them. Their manner with the passengers showed their training and the instilled belief in an elite corps; the glance at the face and clothes, a long, unhurried inspection of the papers and, at last, a flick of the thumb towards the exit. Even the Russian major in front of him received that short, contemptuous gesture.

And now he was with them. Now he was standing before them and they were looking over him with young, efficient eyes that took in everything; the scratch down the side of his face and the stubble on his chin, his stained suit and the weary droop of his body. And now they would know him. The wrecked car must have been found hours ago and, with his knowledge of Russian interrogation methods and Radek's department, and what Radek had threatened to do, they couldn't let him get away.

"Find that man," Radek would have said. "Find him

and bring him back. If you can't bring him back then kill him but, whatever happens, he must not escape."

And now they had found him. Now they had stopped looking at him and the younger and slightly taller of the two had taken his passport, Klee's passport, and was looking at the cover. The boy's nails were long and well-kept as a woman's with the flesh pressed back from the cuticle.

Now he was opening the passport. For the first time on the journey, the book was open and he was reading the words in Russian and German and Polish on the fly-leaf. *The bearer of this document is an official of the State Security Police and must be rendered every assistance in the performance of his or her duty.*

And now he had finished reading and was returning to the second page; the page with the picture. Peter gripped his case as a possible weapon and wondered how far he would get before the dog reached him. He was just about to run when he saw the boy's face alter.

His expression altered completely and it was no longer cold and hard but very warm and full of respect. The respect of a football fan for the international player, the dramatic student for the star, the child for his elder brother.

"Danke, mein Herr," he said and with a little bow handed back the passport.

Very slowly, as though time were unimportant to him, Peter pushed it back into his pocket and gave the boy the kind of look which was expected from him. But, as he stood there, his mind rejoiced and gave thanks. He thanked God for all the luck he had been given and, once more, he blessed the Secret Police for the fear of their name and the power in the paper he carried. Then he bowed back curtly and began to walk forward to freedom. He had taken exactly three steps when he heard the voice.

"One moment if you please, Mr. Carlin."

It was a thick, muddy voice without tone or modulation and it sounded like something rotten breaking in two. Its owner looked just like it.

The man came from behind the barrier and he was short and fat and wore a dark grey suit with food stains down the front. He had a bow tie and the knot was like a button forced into the folds of his thick neck.

"Yes, just one moment please. I rather think you are the person I have been waiting to meet." He pulled a sheet of paper from his pocket and peered at it through pink, short-sighted eyes. Unlike the boy's, his nails were cracked and frayed and there was the dirt of years behind them.

"Quite so," he said, still looking at that paper. "You are the man we want and I have been expecting you. Yes, aged thirty-four but looks rather older—height, five foot eleven inches—weight, one hundred and seventy pounds —hair, dark brown—speaks fluent German but with a slight accent—is possibly carrying the marks of a recent injury.

"Yes, that all seems to fit, doesn't it? And now we will go into my office and try out a little of your fluent German, Mr. Peter Carlin."

Peter hit him. He was tired and his shoulder still ached but he hit him. He hit him with everything he'd got left, with the fury that comes from despair. He swung his case like a pick-axe, aiming for the man's tie, and he might have been splitting the last rock that barred the way to a virgin gold mine. He hit him just where he wanted and felt the case go home, sinking through unhealthy flesh to crush the Adam's apple below. He saw the man reel backwards towards the guards and the dog and the next instant he was running.

He was running through the booking hall, with shouts behind and on both sides of him, but in front and very close was the blue sign of the underground railway. He ran for the entrance beneath the sign, dodging a trolley laden with crates, cannoning against the porter who tried to stop him and, at last, he was on the steps and going down with a rush.

And his luck still held. The woman at the gate drew back before him and there was a train alongside the platform. A bright, yellow train was just drawing away and it was one of the old type with hand-operated doors. He ran beside it, dragging back a door with his left hand while his right grasped the pillar within and pulled himself up towards escape and freedom. It was at that moment the dog had him.

The dog came across the platform in a bouncing, black curve and it knew its business. It paused slightly to judge the distance and then sprang. The teeth closed exactly where they had been trained to close; around his wrist and just below the protection of the sleeve.

But Peter held on. The fangs were fire burning into his arm and the weight was pulling him down but he held on. He clutched the pillar, braced his feet on the step and prayed that the train would not stop.

It didn't. The driver was already screened by the tunnel and he never saw the waved signals or heard the shouts. The non-automatic doors needed no guard to control them and the train put on speed. It came down the platform in a clicking roar, but at the mouth of the tunnel, the police were waiting.

Peter strained against the pull of the dog and he watched them. There were two of them; one with a gun in his hand and the other crouched and ready for a leap at the doorway. With the fangs drawing him out he watched the distance decrease and, when he was almost up to them, he acted. He leaned forward a little more and then arched his body. The big Alsatian came up from the platform and it was like a flail at the end of his arm.

And suddenly he was free. There was a noise of thunder and splintering wood around him but the dog went limp and its jaws parted. Then there were shouts and curses and the thud of bodies meeting and the policemen reeling back before the weight of the dog. And, at last, there was no more grip on his wrist, no jaws holding him and he fell to his knees on the lurching floor of the carriage.

There were half a dozen people in that carriage and five of them didn't look at Peter Carlin as he pulled himself to his feet. Five of them busied themselves with their newspapers, fiddled with their belongings or looked fixedly at the walls of the tunnel. They were neither for nor against him. They just didn't want to be involved.

Five of them did that. The one who made up the half-dozen got up from his seat and walked towards Peter.

He was a tall man, six foot two if an inch, and his terrible leanness made him seem taller. He wore a patch over his right eye and the right-hand sleeve of his musty greatcoat was pinned across his chest. Above it was the yellow and black badge of a cripple.

He looked at Peter Carlin, taking in the greyness of his face and the weariness of his face and the blood dripping from his wrist to the floor and he smiled. It wasn't much of a smile, just a creasing of the mouth and remaining eye, but he tried to make it mean something.

"You are on the run, aren't you, mein Herr?" he said. "You have got on this train because you think it will take you into West Berlin. You are right of course, but you still won't make it. You see, before we reach the frontier, there is one more station in the Russian sector, Unter den Linden, and there they will be waiting for you.

"Yes, at the Linden they will search the train and you have just one chance of escape I think. You will have to walk through them and bluff your way out of the station." He struggled with his left hand and shook the coat from his shoulders. All he had beneath it was a stained, torn shirt which showed the stump of his arm.

"Yes, if you please, take it, mein Herr. I would like you to have it and, with it around you, you might—just might get through. No, please don't argue. There is no time for argument and we are almost there."

And he was right, there was no time. Already the brakes were screaming and the train's motion changing. At any moment they would be among the lights of the station.

Peter didn't look at the man as he pulled the coat round him. It was a dirty, torn coat which smelt stale and musty as though it had lain for years among the rubble. But, all

42

the same, it was the most precious thing he could have given him; probably as precious as life itself.

No, he couldn't look at the man and he couldn't thank him. There was nothing to say which would show his gratitude. He just stood there in that ragged coat, binding a handkerchief round his arm, as the train lurched into the station.

But just before he walked out of the train, the man helped him again. He rested a hand, lean as a child's, on Peter's shoulder and once more he tried to smile.

"No, Mensch," he said, "no thanks. Just get away with it. For that's all the thanks I want. And never feel you owe me anything. What I am doing is for my pleasure alone." He lifted his hand and jerked it backwards towards the East.

"I was there, you see, and I know what it's like. Yes, for fifteen years I was there—after Stalingrad." He turned away, back to his seat, and Peter stepped out onto the platform.

And he did make it. There were police round the train and police at the barriers, but he made it. He walked slowly past them dragging his feet, and they merely glanced at the yellow badge on his chest, the badge of a cripple, and moved aside to let him through. He went up the stairs, holding carefully onto the rail, and he had finished the first stage of his journey.

Outside it was warm and fresh. The southern winds blew through the town and they seemed to dance and ripple through it. The leaves stirred in the trees, screening the rubble, the red flags were just carnival banners and even the unsmiling faces on the political posters seemed to be trying to smile. For he was going home.

He was walking home down the Linden past the motor dealers and the booths selling china and glass and the bookshops with Lenin's picture bright on the dust-jackets. He turned into the Wilhelmstrasse where the new government offices threw a shadow across the site where Hitler had died. And then he was there.

He was just two hundred yards from his destination when he stopped in the Potsdammerplatz. To the right was the exhibition hall and, in front, the gigantic loom of the "H.O."; the co-operative store. There were police standing by the "H.O." and just past them was the frontier board. "YOU ARE NOW LEAVING THE DEMOCRATIC SECTOR OF BERLIN," was written across it.

And, beyond the board, more police were standing. Different police this time; British military police, very smart in their red caps and white piping against the khaki, but still police. And, as he looked at them, he remembered some of the things he had forgotten.

All the way, after the car smash, he had forgotten those things. All the way on the hitch-hike to Leningrad, the night on the train and the long moment at the station, he had forgotten them. He had just had one thought; to get back to his own people and, with their help, find out how Susan died.

And now he was standing, looking at those people, and he made no move towards them. He didn't cross the road to the sergeant and say—"My name is Peter Carlin and you want me for the murder of my wife." He would have liked to say that but it was impossible.

For, whoever had killed Susan had played the cards too well. His own fingerprints were on the gun that had killed her and the car in which she had died. A servant who seemed incapable of falsehood had made a false statement and the aces were piled against him. "They have a clearcut case," Radek had said and Radek was probably right. And, unless he could produce an alibi or fresh evidence, they would have no reason to doubt it.

But he had no alibi, no evidence, so he stood looking at the police of his own country, longing to go to them, but knowing it was impossible.

They would be nice to him of course. They wouldn't threaten him with torture but give him cups of tea and listen to his statement and check what he said and half hope to believe him. But, if, at the end, everything against him held together, then they would stop listening.

"This man is not bad," they would say. "He did not betray his country but came back to face the music. In many ways he is a brave and likeable man worthy of respect. All the same, he killed his wife with a firearm and that is still capital murder in England."

Then, one day, he would hear a hush fall in a big room, the settling of chairs, the stilling of coughs, and an old, scarlet judge would begin to sum up.

No, at the moment, he had nothing to hope for from the British police. They were as much his enemies as the blue figures of the "VOPO." He turned away from them and began to walk towards the American sector. And, as he walked, he thought about Berlin as he had once known it.

He remembered the cold and the ruins and the smell of the rubble and the bodies beneath the rubble and the people who stood all day in the food queues and hunted for scraps in the garbage. And for one of those people he had done a favour.

It had been a small, routine favour and the person who had received it had probably died or forgotten or moved away. All the same, it might be his one hope, his one chance of salvation and he had to take it. He walked on, away from the British police, towards the tall buildings of the West.

Herr Judah Schlot smoked a cigar, drank Schnaps and digested the inner organs of beasts and birds.

He sat in a corner of the Altona Bar, well out of the light and the crowd, and he smiled at human depravity. He was a great little smiler and everything amused him —almost everything.

From where he was sitting, the big room opened out like a fan dotted with sequins which were its tables and every table had a telephone. Judah Schlot liked watching the telephones. They seemed neat and efficient to him; the modern approach to an age-old problem. Over the years, he had learned to read the callers' lips and could usually tell what they were saying.

"Is that the very pretty blonde at Number Ten?" a phone would say. "Yes, that's right, I am the military-looking gentleman with the little black moustache at Table Twenty-Two, where I very much hope you will join me."

Yes, Judah liked the telephones. They gave him a kick and confirmed his views on life; that everything could be bought and nothing was sacred. He liked watching the eyes flicking over the room, looking for a pick-up, the fingers dialling and the lips whispering into the mouthpiece. He enjoyed wondering which approach would succeed and which fail. He was rarely wrong in his judgment either.

"Will the old man with the badly-fitting false teeth date the little actress by the band?" he thought. "Possibly as she's been 'resting' for quite some time now. Will that good-looking but very apparent gigolo get off with the banker's widow? Maybe, but not very likely. He seems too obvious—even for her." Yes, Judah got a lot of pleasure from those telephones.

Not that his own ever rang, except by accident, for who would want to date him? He had no illusions about his appearance. An old, bald Jew with three chins and a body like a walrus in a suit which might have been dragged through every gutter in Europe. That suit annoyed the management but, as he tipped well and was a regular customer, they put up with it. Possibly it both annoyed and flattered the customers too.

"Look at him," they would say. "Look at the old brute sitting there and watching us. He comes every week, drinking plain Schnaps and eating some filthy stew they prepare specially for him. And all he does is to watch. Probably it's the only pleasure he has, though. He lives alone with nothing and gets his enjoyment from looking at all us clever, beautiful, fascinating people."

Judah smiled as he thought of that and remembered the big car that waited round the corner, the two Picassos and a Goya in the Grunewald house, the little bag of stones at Zurich and the five million marks to his credit in the Bank für Handel und Industrie.

Yes, Judah liked thinking about these things and he enjoyed the Altona too, with all its sham and noise and intrigue, for it gave him faith in his occupation.

And now the show was going to begin and he always liked the show. There was something about it that contrasted so strongly with what he saw in the room and gave him relief. Blood and Schnaps in his mouth, heat and smoke on his face and, in front, water.

One man sitting alone at an organ, playing popular tunes, while, with each note, a tall jet of coloured water came curving upwards in a dancing, spinning arc. There was a great wonder in his eyes as he watched those tall jets of water.

He pushed back the chair, refilled his glass and prepared to enjoy the show when the phone rang.

"Yes, Table Eighteen," he said, annoyed at the distraction but not caring, not interested, knowing that, as soon as the caller saw his mistake, the line would go dead. He watched the water and waited impatiently for the click of its dying.

But the line didn't die. Instead he heard the operator's voice to show it was an outside call and then another's voice which he seemed to remember but couldn't quite place. He stiffened a little in his chair as the voice gave its name but not very much, for Judah Schlot was quite used to surprises.

"Yes, of course I remember you," he said against the blare of the music. "But it's been a long time, hasn't it, Captain? Don't ask me why but somehow I expected to hear from you again. Yes, I read the newspapers and I know what you've done but there is still a debt to be paid.

"Of course I'll see you but just at the moment I have some rather urgent business to attend to. Very well, at the corner in half an hour. Auf Wiedersehen, Herr Kapitän Carlin." He dropped the phone into its rest and

47

leaned back. Not until the final note died and the last jet of water shrunk to nothing did he ask for his bill.

Peter Carlin was waiting at the corner of Rankestrasse and the Kurfürstendamm. Behind him were the lights of the Café des Westens and, in front, the ruin of the Kaiser Wilhelm Memorial Church, still preserved as a monument to pain. And he looked a little like that church himself, tall and battered and tired; terribly tired. His wrist was bound in plaster and he had discarded the cripple's coat but his eyes were like the eyes of a soldier who had been too long in action.

He didn't look up as the big Rolls stopped before him and then a door opened, an interior light was switched on and he heard the voice of Judah Schlot.

"Will you get in please, Captain," he said. "I think we will drive around for a little." There was a plaid rug over Schlot's knees and he had discarded the cigar for a foul, blackened pipe. He spoke English in a dozen different accents. He might have been born in America of British parents and spent most of his life in Central Europe. There was a plate glass partition separating him from the driving compartment and the chauffeur before it was a full-blooded Negro. He wore a uniform which would have done credit to a field-marshal.

"So, it really is you," said Schlot, leaning back on the cushions. "At first, I thought I might be the victim of a rather dubious practical joke but it seems the phone didn't deceive me. Yes, it is you and you're on the run which means you've come to me for help. To me, Captain Carlin. After fourteen years you come back and trust your life to me; to a man they say is without trust or honour." He smiled as he said that as though his reputation pleased him.

"Yes, I've come to you for help, Herr Schlot. I didn't want to but there is no alternative. You are, quite literally, the only person in the world I can turn to." Peter looked at him through the drifting smoke and the glow from the street lights and the man didn't seem to have changed at all. The heavy face bore the same lines of

48

weary cynicism, the suit looked and smelt exactly the same as the one he had worn when they first met. Even his rank, charred pipe might never have been replaced.

"Yes," he said. "I have put myself in your hands. I know what you are and what your record is but I had to come to you. Once you said you owed me a slight debt but I doubt if you remember that. Just now, on the phone you said you knew what I'm supposed to have done and you could benefit from that knowledge. Yes, if you want to, Herr Schlot, you have only to pull up by the next policeman and reap many golden opinions."

Schlot laughed. He laughed from deep down in his big body and his chins shook as though carved from lumps of tallow which were beginning to melt.

"Good boy," he said. "Very good. Golden opinions from the police, eh. You know I could never give you up after saying that, so you mention it straight away. Yes, you've become wise since we first met in your British H.Q. so many years ago." Schlot reached out and tilted Peter's face to the light. His hand looked as though it had been torn by a machine which was exactly what had happened to it.

"No, don't worry, I won't give you up, Captain Carlin. Herr Kapitän Peter Carlin, the gallant soldier with the stars and ribbons who once did an old Yiddish crook a service.

"And now still a soldier but quite different. A soldier who is on retreat, eh, Captain? A very, very tired soldier." His eyes watched the pain in Peter's face and then flicked down to his wrist.

"Yes, a wounded soldier who is on retreat and has had no grub, no sleep and a hell of a lot of pain. I know those signs for I've seen men who have been on the run from half the stinking prisons in the world. In Quentin I've seen them, and Dartmoor, and Capodistria Island and Dachau; yes, many of them from Dachau." He knocked his pipe out on the window as he spoke.

The car had left the centre of the town now and they were running through ill-lit, deserted streets. Schlot pressed a button by his arm-rest and the Negro chauffeur braked hard before a little café.

"But I know an antidote for your troubles too. A temporary one of course but it is very simple. Just Schnaps —Schnaps and Wurst and then lots more Schnaps. Come on, let's try it." He climbed heavily out of the car and led the way to the café. It was empty of customers and very small. Just a Bierstube with blue tiles on the walls and a blue stove in the corner. The waitress who took his order bowed deeply to Schlot. She was one of the most beautiful girls Peter had ever seen.

And not till he had watched Peter eat the sausage she put before him, and drunk three glasses of the grey, smoking "Klare," did Schlot speak again.

"Well, Captain, what are we to do with you? You are on the run and you need help. So, you've come to me, haven't you? That was a wise move on your part because I have so many friends—oh, so many." He smiled slightly as he said that.

"So don't worry. We are quite safe here and I've read the papers and know what they say you did. That you killed your wife and sold certain information to the Bolsheviks. Apparently the last is untrue or you would hardly be here.

"Not that it matters to me, of course. We Jews have many faults and perhaps very few virtues. Two of those virtues remain constant however; we pay our debts and we stand by our friends, Captain Carlin.

"And it seems I have a debt to you. Once you showed me a kindness and that must be repaid whether you are a traitor and a murderer or not." He used the words without hint of accentuation as though they were just words to him. As though betrayal and murder and all the mire of human frailty were so ordinary, so common-place, that they were just a bore—just words which conveyed nothing at all.

"Tell me something though. Whatever you answer, please remember that I'll still help you. I just want to

50

know for my personal interest. When you killed your wife, did you hurt her a great deal?"

"Hurt her?" Peter's head jerked back as though Schlot had struck him.

"No," he said, "I didn't hurt Susan. I didn't hurt her for the simple reason that I never touched her. Whatever you've read. Whatever you may think now. I swear that I did not kill my wife."

He leaned forward across the table, looking into Schlot's eyes; those hard eyes that had seen everything, grown tired of everything, and he told his story. He told it slowly and carefully, trying to make every word count because, whether Schlot helped him or not, he had to try and convince him.

He told him of his life after the army and Toni Marric with his touch of genius and how they had met and started the firm together. He told him about Susan and her background and their marriage and her father's warning and how, one day, he had come home and found that Susan had changed.

He told him of the circuit that Toni had planned and the trip to Russia to sell office machinery, because the firm needed money, and the things he had learnt in Russia. How somebody had switched his car without altering the fingerprints and killed Susan with his gun and made Ethel Sommers, the loyal servant, lie.

Then he talked about Radek and the man Radek handed him over to, and the car leaving the road north of Pushkin Village and the long journey to Berlin and the struggle at the station. He passed over that very quickly because somehow it didn't seem important any more. It was all too close and the present did not matter now. Only the past and the future mattered because they added up to one thing—the face of the person who had killed his wife.

But, when he had finished, Judah Schlot's expression didn't alter. He looked just the same as before, bored and unbelieving and cynical. He fiddled for a moment with his pipe, knocking the bowl on the table and scraping it out with a penknife. The knife handle was engraved gold of a heavy carat but he twisted the blade into that filthy pipe as though it had been bought for pennies at Woolworth's.

"Thank you for giving me a picture of your life after you left Berlin," he said, when the pipe had been cleaned to his full satisfaction.

"I am glad you did so well in business, because I like businessmen. I try to pretend that I am one myself. Yes, that part of the story interested me but nothing else did.

"For, as I said before, I neither believe nor doubt you. In fact I am quite without interest in what you have done or not done. I merely asked you if you hurt your wife because I dislike wanton cruelty. And, in any case, I wish to repay my debt. That is what you've come for, isn't it, Herr Kapitän Carlin?" He pushed the pipe back in his pocket and rubbed a thick and not too clean finger across his eyes and the bridge of his nose; a finger in the pie—a nose for a deal—make me an offer—twenty percent and no risk of capital depreciation.

"Yes, I've come to you for that, Herr Schlot. As you say I once did you a favour and now I need your help. If you can give it, that is."

"If I can?" Schlot smiled and lifted his glass. "It rather depends on what you want, of course, but I think I can help you. And I like your coming to me, you know. The whole world against you, all the forces of the East and West on your heels, and only one friend to turn to; Old Judah Schlot, the man who sells everything.

"But don't worry, my dear. I can help becuse I have a world too. A great big world and it's all mine to do what I like with." He looked through the clear liquid in his glass and he seemed to see that world of his. An empire of contacts and meeting places and shady deals that ran across the face of Europe.

He thought of the motor boats drifting in on the swell from Tangier. The lorries with their false tanks grinding north towards Figueras and the French frontier. The lean, brown men mincing down the Southampton gangways with pouches beneath their belts. He considered a commercial gentleman, traveller in toilet preparations, squeezing a tube in Antwerp and watching the diamonds glisten through the soap.

"Before we talk business, tell me something though. You couldn't have known that I still used the Altona, so how did you manage to find me?" He nodded slowly and sadly at Peter's explanation as though he had expected the worst.

"I see. You looked up my name in the phone book and when you rang a man told you I would be there. A pity. That man was my butler and he had orders to tell nobody of my whereabouts. He was a good butler but, it seems, a fool. Now he will have to look for another job.

"Yes, I have a butler, Captain Carlin and I've come a long way since I stood outside your office in the Fehrbelliner Platz. When was that again? Yes, February '46 and you gave me my house back didn't you? It had been stolen by the Nazis and then requisitioned by your army. But you, the officer in charge of these things, let me have it again. I often wondered why you did that, you know. Did you perhaps see the goodness shining through my rather battered exterior?"

"No, I'm afraid it was nothing like that," Peter smiled slightly as he looked at those dark, shifty eyes which shone with nothing except self-interest.

"Strangely enough I felt I was doing my duty. I didn't know what you were then and I felt sorry for you. Besides, the house was clearly your property and the army had no further use for it. There was no reason why it should not be handed back to you. Still, I'm glad you took it as an act of personal friendship."

"So that was it. Just the conscientious British officer doing his duty, eh, Captain. Not for the sake of my bonny, brown hair. All the same, we became friends afterwards, didn't we, and that house put me on my feet again." He paused for a moment and considered how he had climbed back onto those feet; a few tins of coffee, a few bags of sugar, a few cartons of cigarettes. And lastly somewhere to store them. A house in a city where nobody had houses. The little base that had led to an empire.

"And now, let's forget the past and get down to facts." He drained his glass in a single, practiced movement and leaned back; the efficient businessman preparing the way to a deal.

"And the facts are that you must get out of Berlin at once. Up to now, you have been lucky, incredibly lucky, but I don't think that luck will hold out much longer.

"You see, I know our friends behind that 'curtain' and they are a hard, vindictive people. You have learned their secrets and hurt their pride and they won't rest till they get you. At this moment, every agent, every informer they have in Berlin will be looking for you. And, if they find you, I promise there won't be any more car crashes or lucky escapes down the underground railway.

"And what about your fellow countrymen? Just now they think you are safely in Russia but that won't last for long. People have eyes, and your picture has been well displayed in the press.

"Yes, soon they'll know you're back and then the whole pack will be after you. All the world on your heels except an old Yid for whom you once did a favour.

"But, don't worry. The Yid has lots of friends and he'll look after you. All over the earth I have contacts and you can rely on Old Uncle Judah Schlot." He reached deep into the folds of his horrible suit and pulled out a leather-bound book. It was a comfortable-looking, little book, well rubbed and homely and might have held the accounts of a prudent householder, the jottings of the small investor.

"And you can help me too. You are obviously a resolute man and I seem to remember you speak Spanish as well as German. A useful gift is the ability to pick up languages, my dear—very useful.

"So I think that Spain is the place for you. I have certain business interests in Barcelona and Barcelona used to be a nice town. From Mount Tibidado you can see all the way to Majorca on the one side and the holy hill of Montserrat on the other.

"The Spanish police are nice fellows too. Though inclined to harshness with political offenders, they are surprisingly lenient towards legitimate businessmen. Yes, I think we can help each other in Barcelona."

As though struck by a sudden idea, Schlot snapped his fingers at the girl behind the counter. She came towards him at once and he grinned at Peter and admired the swing of her body as though it were a rare and valuable piece of merchandise. Then he dismissed her with a gentle pat across the buttocks.

"And Gerda, here, can go with you. The journey will be easier for two and Gerda is a good, clever girl who tells me she is tired of Germany.

"Yes, that is a good idea, I think. Both of you can look after my interests in Barcelona." He refilled the glasses once more and held out his own to Peter, smiling as he did so; a deep, fishy smile that had taken generations of furtive dealings to produce.

"A toast now, Herr Kapitän," he said. "That things may be pleasant in Barcelona."

But Peter didn't smile in return. He drank a little Schnaps and then put down the glass and shook his head.

"Herr Schlot," he said slowly, "remember that I know you. I was in Berlin for six months after that house transaction and I studied you. Somehow you fascinated me and I felt we had become friends. But, all the time I watched you and pried into your life and I know some of the filthy business you are mixed up in. All the same, I thought you were a man who would keep his word. And, after that house was given back to you, you made a promise. You said that if ever I needed help, in any way, you would give it.

"Well, I'm asking for help now and it has nothing to do with hiding in Spain. I don't want a job in your organization and I don't want a woman. All I want is a passport and a single ticket to London."

"You want that!" Schlot's glass banged down on the table and some of the liquid slopped across the wood. "You want that I should help to hang you, boy." There was suddenly a great wonder in his eyes as though he couldn't understand human reasoning.

"You mean that you were telling me the truth just now? That you really didn't kill her and now you want to go back to England to find who did?" He pulled the pipe from his pocket and wedged it between his teeth. Somehow it seemed to hold the face together.

"Well, don't do it, my dear. I've read the papers and your police think they have a cast-iron case against you. They'd never have allowed the details to be published if they weren't sure.

"And do you know what that means? It means that, whoever killed your wife, has all the cards on his side—every card in the pack. You told me that nobody hated your wife and you have no idea who killed her. Well, I have and it was someone with time and money and brains at his or her disposal; a lot of brains and a lot of power. He is a man with an organization, in fact, who buried you alive in Russia. A man rather like myself. Do you honestly think you would have a chance against such a man?" He waved aside Peter's reply and went on. His words were a mixture of threat and plea.

"No, you'd have no chance. That man would have prepared for everything—even for your return. He's run rings round the police and he'll go on doing so. They'll pick you up within five minutes of your returning to England and then you'll hang. Believe me, with the best passport in the world, they'll pick you up.

"And I don't want that. Even apart from the business of the house I have a fondness for you and I want to help. So do me a favour. Remember what the Christian prophet said—'Let the Dead bury their Dead.' Think about that and go to Spain with Gerda." He watched Peter's face and suddenly a flicker of anger crept across his own.

"All right then. Go to England and hang and be damned to you. But go without my help. Just walk out of

56

here and find a policeman and tell him who you are. In that way, you will at least have the chance of a fair trial.

"Go it alone though—just go home alone on false papers and nobody will listen to you and you'll have not one person to turn to. Think of that for a moment and then consider my offer and go to Barcelona."

"No, no police and no more running." Peter pushed aside the bottle that Schlot held out to him and eased back his chair. He had little hope of making Schlot understand him but he had to try.

"Can't you see it?" he said. "Can't you understand that, at this stage, I dare not give myself up? Somebody killed my wife, and without further evidence, the police are bound to believe I did it.

"And so, I've got to find that person. Even if it costs me my life, I've got to find him. He killed Susan and left me to rot in Russia and I'm going after him. I'm going to find him and take him apart and look him in the face and see what makes him tick. And, if you won't help me, Herr Schlot, I'll go on alone."

"All right, all right, boy. You've made your point and I'll help you to hang yourself, if that's what you want. Now, take your drink and listen to me." Schlot tilted the bottle over his glass and he didn't speak for a moment. He looked at the man who was giving up his life and he thought of his own life and the sins and crimes and stupidities that had forged it.

He thought of a collier called *Molly L* coming up to Key West against the stream; legitimate cargo on deck, gin crates in the hold and a "flammenwerfer" for good measure in the port lifeboat. He remembered how the car had stopped in Bond Street and the boy who was trained like a soldier going through the actions; "One —Smash, Two—Grab, Three—Away." But he'd been a little slow on the last movement because the safety curtain had come down and crushed his hand.

And the last memory was the worst of them all. The guard-room at Dachau and a prisoner who wore the Star of David on his tunic standing by a table. "Herr Major," that prisoner had said, "I have information to give you." "Herr Kommandant, I think I know where the man, Jacob Leuin, hid his gold." "Herr Sturmführer, it is behind the false wall in a basement at 34, Kanstrasse."

He turned away from the memories of his bad life and watched Peter Carlin, seeing the pain in his face and the anger in his face and the slow growth of mania that was welding it together. Then he opened his little leather-bound book.

"Yes, I'll help you, though it's a fool I am and this is poor business. Somebody once said that Old Judah Schlot was so hard, so bad, that he'd do anything for business—that he'd sell his own daughter for a pfennig. Well, that may be right, but it was impossible. My daughter was a remarkably ugly and moral woman.

"And now, you come to this bad man, Schlot, and ask him to repay a small favour from a long time back. You won't do anything for Schlot in return though. You won't go and work for him in Barcelona with a very pretty girl.

"No, nothing in return. All you want is for me to send you back to England where you will certainly hang." He had found what he wanted in his book now and started to scrawl something on a beer mat.

"All right, I'll do what you want. You can go home and hang and rot in hell for all I care. And I will do it, not to pay back a debt but just because it amuses me. Yes, it amuses me to see the once-so-grand, British officer begging me to help him die." As he watched Schlot, Peter suddenly saw that the man was pleading; old, shifty eyes pleading to retain a reputation for wickedness.

"And now to business. You need a passport, a ticket, via the long tourist route, Hanover, Paris, Boulogne, if you are to stand a chance, and money—plenty of money." There was a slight sadness in his voice as he said that.

"Well, you shall have it for I am rather like an army officer too. I say to one man 'come' and to another 'go', and they do what I tell them. There is one man in Berlin now who will help us. He seems a rich, important man who always stays at the best hotels and is a director of a firm producing synthetic sausage skins.

"Yes, an important man on the surface; but when I say to him, 'Mr. George Henderson, I would like to borrow your passport,' he will come running with it."

Schlot had finished writing now and he held out the mat to Peter. The words were in large copper plate as though formed by a school-child.

"And this is the address of another friend of mine. Her name is Lotte Steiner and she runs a private hotel near Tempelhof. Ja, a very private hotel, full of pretty girls dressed in muslin or nothing at all. You should enjoy yourself there, I think; the last fling of the condemned man, eh, Captain.

"I am leaving you now and give me ten minutes to contact Lotte. Then go to her and she will fit you up with the things you want; a ticket, money and a passport with your picture in it. Not that the picture will help you much though. Just let them take a good look at you and you are finished. And no thanks, please. You are a fool, my friend, and I don't want your thanks; though I shall be interested to read of your hanging."

Schlot pushed the book away and slowly dragged himself to his feet. He was about to turn from the table when a strange expression came into his face; the look of a terrier smelling the rat, the prospector seeing the first blue-clay formations of a diamond pipe.

"Herr Kapitän," he said, "you told me how you got out of Russia but you did not say with what. And I can smell something, you know—something which might be of value to me. May I have it please? It could just repay me for all the money and risk and trouble I am taking on your behalf. Ah, thank you, thank you very much indeed." The Russian police pass gleamed dully in his hand.

"Yes, this is good. This may be useful. This may unlock quite a number of doors for me. This almost makes me feel like a businessman again." He tucked it carefully away and began to walk towards the door with shuffling, old man's footsteps. Just before he got there, he turned and looked back at Peter.

"Good-bye, my Captain," he said. "It was nice to see you again but a pity about Barcelona. We could have worked well together there and Gerda is a good, clever girl who would make you happy—far, far happier than the memory of a corpse." He pulled open the door and looked out at the big shiny car that waited for him. He seemed an oddly pathetic figure as he stood there; all the wealth and power in his hands and not a single thing he wanted to buy with it.

"Yes, a pity about Barcelona," he said and he was mainly speaking to himself. "All the same, good-bye, Captain Carlin. And good luck, Mr. George Henderson."

The night had swung round to another day, that day was almost spent and dying, when the plane circled the "Funkturm" and headed for Western Germany.

Schlot stood below the radio tower and watched the plane fade into the distance. Though he believed in nothing there was almost a prayer on his lips as he watched it. The prayer stopped abruptly as he saw the car pull up at the curb and the men come towards him.

There were two men and they looked identical. One was tall and middle-aged and the other young and running to fat but something about them made them look the same. They raised their hats and nodded politely as they stopped before him.

"Herr Judah Schlot," said the older of the two and his question was quite rhetorical. "Will you come with us please as I rather think you may have some information we need?

"And don't try anything, will you? I know we are in the Western Sector of the city but don't try to run or cry out or ask for help." He moved slightly to one side so that Schlot could see the gun bulging in his companion's pocket.

"Yes, that's right, we are intelligence officers of the East German Peoples' Republic."

CHAPTER FOUR

"THANK you, Mr. Henderson. And you are visiting this country for pleasure, I understand?"

The official took the passport, feeling the cloth worn smooth by a hundred frontiers and squinted at the seal and the writing across it. *I Secretary of State—John Foster Dulles request—*Then he looked at the photograph and its owner's particulars.

Yes, everything was in order. "George T. Henderson—U.S. citizen—Born, Boston, 1923—Occupation, Independent."

Just so, "independent." The stamps and the visas bore that out and proclaimed the book a rich man's companion on his journeys across the world; Mexico, Monaco, Bermuda, Germany and France.

Very nice too, but the rich man had been beating it up on his travels. He looked at the lines on the face and the tiredness of the face and, for a second time, there seemed something familiar about the man. He held the stamp over the page, trying to place his face, but, when he did, he smiled to himself. For it was just a resemblance. It had to be a resemblance.

The man Henderson looked like would never return to England. As far as the West was concerned, that man was dead. He pushed the thought away from him, brought the stamp hard down and considered his own frugal holidays in Southport; the house with the increased mortgage, four kids and a wife to keep, eighteen pounds a week and glad to get it.

"Thank you, sir," he said hating that lined, familiar

face which good living and good money had made. "And I hope your stay in this country will be very pleasant."

"And thank you, I'm very sure it will be." Peter Carlin tucked the book back into his new, off-the-peg but quite reasonable suit, concentrating on keeping the slight drawl in his voice, and stepped out through the partition into the rain.

And somehow the rain was the homecoming he needed. English spring rain drifting in over the white cliffs from the "Downs" behind and the little fields and the beech woods and the big city to the north; rain which seemed to wash away the tiredness and agony of the last three weeks.

He stood for a moment outside the customs shed, feeling the rain soft on his face and smelling damp grass mingling with salt-spray and sea-weed iodine. Beside him, the young lady in the cigarette kiosk confided to a friend.

"And I looked him right in the eye and said, 'Mr. Jackson, you can't speak to me like that.' And do you know what he replied? 'Very well, Miss Hawks, if I can't, you can get the hell out of here.'"

Peter grinned as he listened to her and then walked through to the station and the Pullman car which would take him to London.

And, as he climbed into it he knew he was home. He leaned back on the thick cushions, taking in the heavy brass lamps and the winking mirrors, and knew it was part of him.

For "home" wasn't just a word or a sentiment to dream or sing about: *Rule Britannia, There'll always be an England*. White cliffs rising grandly out of the sea as bastions of freedom. Home was thin rain on his face, the complaining chatter of girls and the little, overheated, hurrying trains of his youth.

But, though he was home, he was not yet welcome. He looked at the faces of his fellow travellers for a moment; bored, tired, disinterested faces, just now, but they could be different. Only let them recognize him and they wouldn't be bored any more.

"That's him," they would say. "That's Carlin, the murderer, the traitor, the one who sold his country, the man we're looking for—" He turned away from the thought of hatred and rage lighting up those bored, mild faces.

Not that it was likely they would recognize him of course. As far as England was concerned, Peter Carlin was dead—dead and done with. Besides, the pictures in the press had showed a well-built man in his early thirties. Now his face was lean and haggard and middle-aged, while the hair brushed back gave it a cheap and slightly shabby appearance.

Schlot's friend, Lotte Steiner, had done that for him. Lotte did some clever hairdressing in her brothel behind Tempelhof and she was clever in other ways too. It was Lotte who had planned the route home for him. All the way round via Paris and Boulogne so he could mingle with the holiday crowds.

But now he was home, with the real work before him, and there was no Lotte or Judah Schlot to help. He was quite alone; Ulysses on the shore of Ithaca with nothing to support him except the great, pounding hate in his heart.

And that was wrong because Ulysses had had the old fisherman, the faithful hound and his dream of Penelope. He had no dream, no Penelope, for Susan was dead. She was dead and buried by now; laid out in the Guilford vault; killed by a gun which bore his fingerprints, in a car that he knew was parked at the airport.

He looked out of the window at the hurrying fields of England and he tried to think of the girl he had married. After a time he gave it up because he had two pictures of her and neither of them fitted.

For, though Susan had been a good wife to him, he'd never really known her. He couldn't have done, or he would have persuaded her to tell him about the thing that terrified her. And something had done that.

For who is one person today and changes tomorrow? Who is a wife for two years and, though you don't really understand her, seems happy and gay and loves and laughs

63

and then, one day, withers at a moment's notice? Who kissed you good-bye in the morning and when you came home was a different woman you've never seen before? Answer, Mrs. Susan Carlin.

Oh, yes, she'd changed. He remembered that night, three months ago; the key in the door, his feet on the hall and a shout of greeting. But nobody to answer him except a grey, frightened face turning away and a voice he'd never heard before saying, "Leave me alone—Please, please leave me alone."

Well, he'd done that. He'd thought it was nerves at first and waited for her to come back to him. And at the very end, when she might have come back, he'd failed her. He'd seen her eyes, begging him to stay while he packed his case, but he'd let her down. He'd gone out of the flat and driven to Gatwick by way of the factory and left her alone with the maid and the knowledge that she was to have a visitor.

And the end of his journey had been a walk to the Neva Bridge, a hand on his shoulder and the world turning round, trying to straighten, but never quite doing so. And, at last, a man called Radek sitting at a desk drawing animals on his blotter.

But who could have killed Susan? Who would have wanted to? What had happened to her that day and brought her back a stranger? And who was the person who knew so much about his movements? That he had planned to leave the flat at nine and go round by the factory—that Toni Marric was building a certain piece of equipment the Russians would like to know about—that he would park the car at the airport and there was a revolver in the glove pocket of that car?

And there were just two people who knew the answers to all those questions; Toni Marric and Susan herself.

Yes, Susan had known those things and the look in her eyes had been part plea, part warning. She'd wanted to tell him the truth but she hadn't been able to. Was she just frightened to tell him or was it from a quite different reason? Was it her centuries-old pride that had stopped her? Would she, quite literally, die, rather than tell him that?

For a moment he tried to think of that pride of race and name which might have kept her silent, but his whole background revolted against it and made it meaningless.

Her father for instance, he'd never understood her father. An old, tired man who fought to hold his body straight against the injury he had received on the hunting field thirty years ago. An old man, obsessed by blood and tradition, who ran his estate like a feudal baron but had another side to him. A man who had a deep sense of guilt for all the things his family had taken and struggled to pay them back through charity; prisoners' aid and housing, child welfare and moral reform.

Peter remembered Walter Rayne standing in his dark study with a single lamp playing on the books which were family histories, county annals and genealogies—Debrett and Burke, Fox Davis and Cockayne.

"We are an old, old family, Mr. Carlin," he had said. "The Raynes were people before the Cecils were thought of and our banners stood with the Hunchbacked Richard at Bosworth Field. On the whole I am proud of my family but, of some things they did, I am not so proud.

"This very lovely house, for example, was built by monies paid to my ancestor by Sir John Hawkins, the great slave trader. The name of Hawkins' ship is interesting; it was the *Jesus*.

"During the eighteenth century, we Raynes enclosed some six hundred square miles of common land in East Anglia and left the tenants to starve. During the nineteenth, a thousand children must have died in our Lancashire mines.

"And, because I am proud of my name, I want to pay back a little of what some of us stole. Can you understand that, Mr. Carlin? Can you understand that I have two duties in life; to preserve this estate in spite of taxes and death-duties and, by what sentimental fools call 'good

65

works,' to pay back some of the things my family took?"

No, Peter Carlin, the self-made businessman, couldn't understand that and all his instinct turned away from the worship of the past. And, in any case, the Rayne family were finished now. Sir Walter's only relative, a nephew, had never seen death as it came to him from a German cruiser's first salvo. Susan lay in the Guilford vault. There was no one left to carry on the name.

Yes, the Raynes were finished with their dream of greatness and guilt and pride. And because of that pride, because his wife had been too proud or frightened to speak, he might well be finished too.

The train was running into London now. Fields and trees were giving way to steel and brick and concrete and the rain had stopped. Red buses ran across a bridge parallel to the line and, in the corner of a park, three children played with a yellow dog. Even against the checked rattle of the wheels, he could hear their voices, shrill and slightly hysterical through the damp air.

And, somehow, those children reminded him of Susan; for she had played like that, a little too keenly and too hard. The hands white and clenched on the wheel as the big car hurled itself down Route Nationale 10, the body tense on a Scottish grouse moor and the eyes concentrating a little too much as she waited for the tennis service.

Even at the end, when she drew away from him, that tenseness remained. He remembered her at night, sitting under the bed light, while her hand gripped a pencil as it travelled across the diary he was never allowed to see.

And that diary was the thing he had come back to find. It was a hundred to one against his finding it of course and it was probably of no importance. The police had most likely discovered it weeks ago and it would contain nothing to help him.

All the same, he had to go back and look, because that little book might hold the thing he wanted—the name of a killer. Even though he was putting his head through a noose he had to try and find it.

He pushed back the door as the train coughed to a halt

and began to walk briskly up the platform. Just beyond the barrier was a post box and he stopped beside it to fulfil a promise.

He took out the envelope he had filled in on the boat and sealed it over the passport that Schlot had "borrowed" for him. He smiled slightly as he looked at the address of the person who was to return it to Henderson. "The Rev. Canon Gore-Brown, The Old Vicarage, Derington near Colchester." Then he crossed to the cab rank.

He was very tired as he leaned back in the taxi and fear was like a cloud around him. For, though his trail might be well hidden, the pursuers could not be too far behind. Schlot's offer of Barcelona suddenly seemed very attractive.

But, as the cab rolled on through the evening traffic, his mind relaxed a little because he was going home. He was going back to the place where it had all started and truth might be found.

At the same time, home was the one place where they would be bound to recognise him.

And in Berlin, Judah Schlot was thinking about Barcelona as well.

Barcelona seemed not only attractive to him but a haven of peace; the very Islands of the Blessed.

He sat with his palms spread open on his plump knees and looked round the room which had once been his joy and pride. He saw the Persian rugs on the parquet floor, heavy furniture of plush and gold, an inlaid Bechstein piano with "Lazarus Risen" by Goya behind it and, below the Goya, his choice collection of Fuseli engravings.

Once, that room had given him so much pleasure and warmth; the crux of a life's endeavour, the climax of a hundred crooked deals. Now it seemed merely trash and he was just a fat, obscene, old man who had aged overnight.

And it was the way they turned him out that had broke him. If it had been done differently he might have stood it, might have put up with it and preserved some slight vestige of respect, but their dismissal had been quite stark, even lacking the interest of contempt. The information peeled from him as by a plane through soft wood and a man who didn't bother to look up from his notes pointing to the door.

"Yes, that is all, Herr Schlot and we won't detain you further. You have been most co-operative and I don't think you will mention this interview to anyone. No, I don't think you will do that." There had been no threat in his words; merely certainty.

At the beginning, Schlot had tried to hold out, of course. He was an old, old hand at police interrogations and, when they first took him in, he felt quite confident; playing for time, hedging and denying that he'd ever known a man named Carlin.

"But this is quite absurd, gentlemen. I have read about this man Carlin in the papers of course, but I've never met him. Now you say I was seen, in his company, by one of your agents. We were going into a certain café in the American Sector.

"Well, it's quite untrue, gentlemen. And why should I want to help a person like that—an accused murderer. I am a man of some standing in this city. I own three businesses and I don't know how many houses. What would I be doing with anybody like Carlin?"

Yes, Schlot had done his best, and, with Western police, he might have stalled or even got away with it. These weren't Western police, however, and their methods were rather different.

They'd put their questions most politely, smiled a little at his heated denials, and acted. A hand had reached out and taken his in a grip which seemed pleasant and friendly, holding it as though exploring its shape and texture. Then, in a single expert movement, it had hardened, bent back and broken his little finger.

Schlot talked. He wasn't a coward but physical pain was something he couldn't face, couldn't stand up to. He looked at his finger hanging slack and loose, like a folded handkerchief, and he talked. He told them about Peter, and the passport he had given Peter, and that Peter was on his way back to London. He told them everything they wanted. Then, with fire in his hand and water in his eyes, he walked out into the street.

And now, he was finished with Berlin. He looked at the room which had once given him pleasure but knew it was stale and he would have to leave it for a time. He took a map from his big desk and spread it out in front of him. The blue of the seas, especially the southern seas, looked beckoning and attractive.

Yes, he would go away and try to forget. He thought of long beaches and warm water and the rustle of palm trees behind him. He tried very hard to think of those things, but he couldn't really concentrate.

All the time, his eyes kept flicking north to a certain dark speck on the canvas; to the town of London where the net would be closing in round the man he had betrayed.

CHAPTER FIVE

VANESSA COURT stands at the top of the Gloucester Road where Kensington proper meets the Park and withers before Bayswater and Notting Hill.

The block is quite small; only four floors, twelve flats and a single rickety lift presided over by a decrepit hall porter. All the same, it is very, very select. Only the "best" people live there and, when they die, great care is taken to find acceptable replacements. It was only through her father's name that Susan had managed to take a lease three years ago. It was a lawyer's lease too and, on her death, would have died with her.

Peter stood back, out of the beam of the street lamp, and looked at the entrance. He felt strange standing there, as though the events of the last weeks had never happened. The days might have run back, the time might be just after seven and he was on his way home from the factory.

He would walk in through the swing door with his case in his hand, nod to old Hodgson, the porter, and, if he remembered, ask how his rheumatism was. Then, he would go up in the creaking lift to the third floor; to the cold kiss on the cheek from Susan, the supper prepared by Ethel Sommers, the drab return to a marriage which had ceased to exist.

But the days had passed, the time was not seven but nine-thirty and nobody he knew would be in the flat to wait for him. The police must have gone through it with a fine-tooth comb weeks ago and left. After all, the case was closed, he was known to have fled to Russia, and there would be no point in keeping a watch on it longer.

Susan's solicitors would have handed the lease back to the landlord who would have started looking for a new tenant. It might take him a little time to find one however. Though no actual killing had taken place there, the flat was associated with murder and the "best" people dislike scandal.

And now he was going back to it; back to the scene of his supposed crime, as all killers are supposed to do. He prayed that the police had not found everything, that the flat was not let, that old Hodgson had gone "round the corner" for one of his incessant glasses of mild-ale, and walked quickly through the door.

And in the phone box across the street, a middle-aged woman stopped fiddling in her bag for change and watched him go. She was a very ordinary-looking woman in a faded blue coat and she might have been the wife of an artisan, or small shop-keeper, ringing up her married daughter in Birmingham. The eyes that looked at him from behind her National Health glasses were very bright and intelligent and they didn't miss a thing.

But his luck was still holding out. No bent figure sat behind the porter's desk, and the lift was on the ground floor, ready and waiting. He stepped into it, pressed the third button and, for the hundredth time, wondered when the worn blue carpet would be replaced. Then, as the machine stopped, he pulled back the door and walked out before the flat where he had last seen his wife.

And, as he had prayed, it seemed that no new tenant had moved in. No light came from behind the door and his own name plate still shone on the lintel. With just a little more luck, he might search undisturbed for the thing he wanted.

He glanced round the landing for a second and then pulled a nail file out of his pocket; for he knew that door well. Once, he had come home without a key on the maid's night-off, and discovered the gap in the frame, where a piece of steel or stiff celluloid could press back

71

the lock; how many times he had intended to get it repaired.

He fiddled with the file, forcing it home between the shrunk wood, and felt it go through, touching nothing at all. Somebody had left the door unlocked then. He pushed it open and walked into the darkened hall. At that moment, his luck ran out.

The first thing he saw was the bird. It stood against the window, outlined by a street light, and it was a big, big bird which would have reached up to his chest. Its plumage was shabby black, with an obscene ruff round the neck, and the head was bald and carried a long bill the colour of dull slate. Its expression was one of the most evil things he had seen on a living creature and it didn't seem to like the look of him either.

It drew back slightly, lowered its head and started to come forward with a walk which was both strut and threat. Then, behind it, a voice rang across the room; a loud booming voice that might have come from the lips of an ogre.

"Just who the hell are you and how dare you enter my flat without knocking?" The door of the sitting room was partly open and a thin beam of light came from it which he hadn't seen on the landing. Through that gap, deep and domineering, the voice rolled towards him.

"Well, are you coming in, or do you expect *me* to come out and fetch you? It will be much worse for you if I have to." The rasping arrogance of the voice seemed to shake the entire building.

For a second, Peter stood quite still, preparing to bolt before that terrible voice, but somehow he couldn't. He had done with running now and come too far. Whoever there was behind that door had to be faced.

"Oh, I see. You're frightened of Wellington, are you? No need to be, just kick the brute out of the way and come through. He's a Jabiru, a South American stork, and one of the most friendly chaps alive—at least when I'm around."

"Very well, I'm coming." Peter edged past the friendly Wellington, keeping well out of range of its razor-sharp bill. On closer inspection, the domed head and little, vicious eyes did bear a slight resemblance to the hero of Waterloo.

"Yes, that's better and now I can have a look at you." The owner of the voice lolled back in the one comfortable chair in the room, and, all around him, there were trunks and packing cases and pieces of outlandish equipment.

Behind the chair, a red shaded lamp lit him up like a television announcer and he was big and hard with muscle and wore a suit of surprisingly vulgar check. His enormous head was bald and the flowing, ginger moustache of a colour sometimes associated with courage but more often with rank ill-temper. He raised a hand to tilt the lamp at Peter but didn't bother to get up.

"Now, sir. Though I rarely bother to lock my door, it doesn't mean that everybody has the right to walk in. Just who are you and what exactly do you want? By your appearance, one of three things I imagine. A sneak thief who has come for pickings, in the hope the flat was unoccupied; a parasite on society, hoping to sell vacuum cleaners or worthless insurance; a fawning domestic servant who requires employment.

"Well, speak up, man. What exactly do you want?"

Peter thought for a moment before replying, while his eyes swept the litter of the room. There was a trunk in front of him covered with labels and heavy, white letterings. They read "J. Moldon Mott, Esquire, M.A., F.Z.S.", followed by a host of other qualifications which were meaningless to him. Like a gift from space, the makings of a lie came into his mind.

"I was sent round to call on you, Mr. Mott," he said quickly. "I apologize for not knocking, but, as the door was open, I took the liberty to walk in. My name is George Henderson and I'm from the *Courier*. Our editor hoped you might help with a story he wants to run."

"I see, that explains quite a lot. Only a journalist would have the impertinence to behave in the mannerless way you have done.

"Still, from the *Courier*, eh. Not a bad newspaper, I suppose, in a canting, suburban sort of way." Mr. Mott still scowled, still looked hostile, but not quite as much as before. In fact, an expression which might have been gratified vanity was creeping into his face.

"Yes, I've been expecting one of you chaps to call for some time. For the life of me, I can't understand why it hasn't been done earlier. After all, I've been in residence over three days now and the only reporters I've seen were two scribbling children from the local 'rag.'

"Really most extraordinary. Not only bad manners, but bad business, I should have thought."

"I'm sorry, sir. The fact is the editor thought you should have time to settle in before we bothered you."

"Did he indeed? Most considerate of him. And when he does bother me, he sends somebody round at nine o'clock at night who doesn't even have the manners to knock." He stretched out a hand like a boxing glove and poured some yellowish liquid from a bottle beside him. It smelled strong and horrible.

"Well, since you are here, I'm prepared to grant you an interview. Please remember I'm a busy man though and my time is extremely valuable." He lifted his glass and swallowed the disgusting liquid with every sign of satisfaction.

"One thing puzzles me, however. Why did the *Courier* send you? I know most of their senior reporters and surely one of them should have come; Willis perhaps, or Carmichael or Vernier.

"What did you say your name was? Yes, Henderson—George Henderson, and it rings no bell at all. From your clothes and general manner I should think that you are still at the foot of the profession, though no longer young. Not your fault, I dare say, but it seems strange that they should have sent somebody of your type to interview me."

Peter counted five slowly, before he answered. At the moment, all thought of the murder, all hopes of revenge vanished, and he had just one aim, one ambition in life; to seize this obnoxious person by the seat of his vulgar pants and hurl him to the pavement three stories below. Only two things held him back. In the first place, Mott could give him a good three stone and seemed in the pink of condition. Secondly, the bill of the bird, Wellington, was poised just above his right kidney.

"I'm sorry you feel like that, Mr. Mott," he said, as reason returned, and he fought to make his voice seem meek and respectful. For, whoever this man might be, he was obviously a very queer fish who needed skilful handling.

"The fact is that the editor told me to make a short, preliminary sketch before sending over a senior man. For the sake of my job, I really would be most grateful if you would help me."

"Yes, I bet you would and I suppose one must be charitable. It's probably not your fault you're still a junior and few of us can rise to the great heights of the world." Mott's face suddenly looked quite good-humoured.

"Yes, I'll give you your story, and first I'll give you something else. Before we get down to business, you shall have a treat; something you won't forget in a hurry." He stretched out his hand again and slopped more of the evil-smelling liquid into another glass.

"This is a very special form of alcohol, Mr.—? Thank you, Henderson." Somehow he managed to make the name sound slightly insulting.

"It is probably one of the very few known cases of an animal substance being used as a distilling medium. The Jakuras of Central Mexico make it from sugar mixed with the gall of the Gila lizard. The tribe prize it highly as a notable aphrodisiac. Not that they need much help in that direction." He leered at Peter like a rutting baboon and handed him the glass.

"An old chief gave me this sample last year. As a matter of fact, I had saved his son's life under circumstances of exceptional hardship and danger. The trick is to knock it straight back. Cheers!"

"Cheers!" Peter had to play the game to the end, and very slowly, he forced the glass to his lips. The smell of the stuff was like a dirty drain and quite overpowering. In front of him he could imagine a cageful of Gila Monsters crawling towards his face.

He closed his eyes, held his breath and drank. A second later, something like a red-hot bar seemed to enter his stomach.

"Good God!" The liquid itself had been oily and almost tasteless but the power was behind it. Like a racing car violently accelerated, like the first thrust of a moon rocket, his senses leapt forward, the pain in his stomach died, and everything became glowing and wonderful. He felt that, after another such drink, he would open his eyes and see the true face of God. All he did see was the face of the disagreeable Mr. Mott, but he was full of respect as he looked at it.

"Yes, yes indeed. That is really most impressive. I wonder if I might try one more?"

"Oh, no you don't. For a beginner you've taken that very well, but, any more, and you'll pass out and your paper will lose its story. Besides, that stuff's precious." Mott rammed the cork home and stood up. On his feet, he looked even larger and more aggressive.

"Well, let's go through to my den and have a yarn. It's the only room in this dump I've managed to make habitable yet and we'll feel more comfortable there. Get out of my way, you bastard." He kicked the bird to one side, pounded Peter on the shoulder, and opened the door to what had once been Susan's very feminine bedroom.

And here, the change in the flat was fantastic; for Mott's "den" was a room in name only. It had every element of the madman's horror, the child's nightmare, the cave of the ogre.

Its walls were lined with skulls, some animal, some human, and lights inside them showed to advantage the collection of devil-masks, African drums and dangerously

76

sharp, primitive weapons. As he looked around him, Peter suddenly went quite rigid; for they were not alone in the room.

A few feet away, under the nearest skull-lamp, a man was standing. He was a tall, tall man, seven foot or there-abouts, and coal black. His feet were bare and a faded, khaki great-coat was wrapped around him. On its shoulders, glinting in the dim light, were the red and gold flashes of a brigadier.

"Ahah! I thought that would shake you. Gave the old charwoman near hysterics when she came in this morning." Mott roared with laughter and switched on a light in the ceiling. In its beam, Peter could see the thing was a dummy, but of a kind he couldn't recognise.

"Yes, that's old 'General Poland,' the Mau Mau Communist leader. He gave 'em a run for their money all right; said to have killed over a dozen policemen.

"I was near Mount Kenya at the time—after Rhino, as it happens and, when I heard his band were in the area, I naturally went to look for them. Stalked the blighters for three days and finally got 'Poland' with my Mannlicher Repeater. Lovely, little gun that and a lovely shot, as you can see." He tilted back the head to reveal a gaping rent below the jaw-line.

"As he was one of their biggest chaps in every way, I thought he'd make a handsome addition to my collection. A couple of Masai bearers stuffed the body, and we shipped it home marked 'Botanical Specimens—Fragile —This Side Up' and all the rest of it. What the Customs boys would have said, if they'd opened the crate, I can't imagine. I've had him in store since last week, and only hope the moths haven't got into him." He waved Peter to a bamboo chair and leaned back against the hideous figure.

"Well, Mr. Henderson," he said. "I am now ready for your interview." His manner was that of an eastern potentate conferring an honour on one of his least touchable subjects.

"Thank you, sir." Peter concentrated hard, searching

77

for the right approach. He had no idea who Mott was, or what his story might be, but this was the room he wanted. In this chamber of horrors, which had once been Susan's bedroom, he might find the thing he had come for; a book containing the name of her killer. If he could only play Mott a little more, persuade him to go out of the room, he could start his search.

"Tell me, Mr. Mott," he said. "I understand that you have been here three days now. How did you manage to get the flat? I mean, wasn't it difficult, so soon after the murder? Didn't the police have any objections?"

"The police? Good heavens no, and what a strange question to ask. The police were only too delighted, in fact they helped me. When I got off the boat at Liverpool, I read about the murder and, needing somewhere to live, got in touch with my friend Tom Winterton at the Yard. That's Sir Thomas Winterton, of course, the Assistant Commissioner.

"He took me round to the agents personally and they fixed me up at once. Most delighted to have me, as I'm obviously the right type of tenant. Yes, they were pleased and so were the police.

"You see, it seems that this wretched man, Carlin, fled to Russia and will probably never be heard of again. But, if he did come back, however, if he had the nerve to return to the scene of his crime, as killers are said to do, then he'd find somebody who knew how to deal with him, wouldn't he?"

"Yes, I'm sure he would." Peter glanced at Mott's bulging neck and knotted muscles and turned away his eyes.

"And, since you've been here, sir, have you thought much about the murder? Have you noticed anything the police might have overlooked?"

"Have I noticed anything?" Mott frowned and pulled a cigarette from his case. Then he turned to the stuffed Negro and struck a match on its forehead. It was obviously a common action, for in the light, Peter could see a maze of little shiny lines.

"No, I've noticed nothing," he said angrily. "And what

78

does it matter in any case? I'm quite sure your editor didn't send you here to waste my time discussing this flat or some sordid killing. Let's just get down to Greenland shall we?"

"To Greenland!" Peter's face contorted with surprise and it was one of the worst blunders he had ever made.

"Yes, of course, to Greenland. To my expedition to Greenland. To my discovery of a completely new species of whale. Good God!" Mott stood quite still, breathing deeply, and a dark flush crept over the bald dome of his head.

"So, that's it, is it? Your miserable paper did not send you here to interview me about the expedition at all. You have forced your way in to try and produce some trashy atmosphere story about this flat—about some wretched nonentity who killed his, probably vile, wife and fled to the Bolsheviks.

"And you, you, Mr. Henderson, must be one of the most ignorant and foolish men I have ever encountered. Why, you have never heard of my expedition to North Greenland, have you? You don't even *know* who I am. Well, I intend to show you."

With surprising agility for one of his bulk, he bounded across the room and pulled a pile of books from a packing case in the corner. For a moment, looking at that flushed, angry face, Peter feared he was about to hurl them at him.

Then, the face slowly relaxed and Mott began to smile. It was a small smile, with little good humour in it, but a great deal of pity and contempt; the smile of a space voyager confronted with the denizen of a distant and inferior planet.

"Well, I suppose one must make certain allowances," he said. "You poor scribblers, who spend your lives grubbing for stories in the gutter, must be sadly out of touch with the larger and finer aspects of life. All the same—" The smile turned down at the edges and became the hurt petulance of a spoiled child.

"All the same, I would have thought you'd know some-
79

thing about me. Do you mean to say you've never heard of 'Mount Mott' in Basutoland or the 'Mott River' up by Hudson's Bay? Never read the *works?*" With the gesture of an emperor, presenting his first-born to the assembled multitude, he held out the books.

"These will show you, anyway."

The dust jackets bore the imprint of a sound publishing house and there was no doubt as to their author's identity. On each cover, Mr. Mott scowled forth from a jungle background and he wore shorts, a sun helmet, heavy boots, and a rifle was slung across his shoulder. Behind him, groups of natives stood in attitudes of respect, dread and adoration. The natives varied in colour from brown to black and yellow to khaki, as did the vegetation, but the format of the books remained the same. Peter looked at the bold, black lettering across each volume.

Mott's Wanderings in Central America, he read. *With Mott Across the Lost Kalahari. On the Track of the Abominable Snowman* by J. Moldon Mott. He suddenly recalled a small and disagreeable nephew who owned a collection of such books and set great store by them.

"Yes, yes, of course I realize who you are now." He lied respectfully. "You really must forgive my mistake, but the editor never told me who I would find here. I was merely sent to interview the new tenant of the flat and get his views on the Carlin murder. I never, for one moment, thought I was about to meet *the* J. Moldon Mott."

"No, I suppose you wouldn't if your editor hadn't told you." Mott took the books from him and replaced them in the box. When he walked back, his face looked quite different; heavy and dangerous and scholarly, with little ridges of flesh puckering up over his eyes. A minute before, Peter had felt he was dealing with a self-opinionated buffoon. Now he saw there was nothing comical about the man who was coming towards him.

"No," said Mott and he was very close now with the spread of his shoulders almost reaching Peter's chin. "No, if your editor didn't tell you, you couldn't have known

80

could you? And, in any case, you didn't come to learn about my story, but the Carlin murder—about something that the police may have missed perhaps.

"And it's not for you to apologise to me, but quite the opposite in fact. I called you a fool and I was wrong; completely wrong." His hand came up gripping Peter's arm, and fingers like machines started to kneed and tear into the muscle. However much he strained against them, Peter had no power left to withstand the grip of those terrible fingers.

"Yes," said Mott quietly. "You're no fool and it's not my story we want but yours. Yes, I very much want to hear that story, Mr. Henderson—or should I say, Mr. Peter Carlin?"

CHAPTER SIX

IT WAS the end of the line, for he had given up and told everything and the matter was finished. He sat back in the bamboo chair and waited for Mott to phone the police.

And, part of him was glad that it was all over, that the end had come and he had "thrown in the sponge." For now, there would be no more running, no more pain and no more fear. He was finished with fear, and soon they would come and take him away, and listen very kindly to him, and lock him up. Then, if no more miracles happened, he might one day walk out of a little warm room and hear a clock begin to strike nine.

No, somehow he didn't care at all. The thought of death meant nothing to him, though he would have liked to see the face of the person who killed Susan. Yes, he would have liked that, but he had no more energy left to fight on. All his energy had been drained away during the days in Russia, the journey across Europe and the last hour in this dark, trophy-hung room. He just couldn't go on any further, so he waited impatiently for Mott to go to the phone.

But Mott made no move at all. He leaned back against the tall figure of "General Poland" and added another cigarette stub to the growing circle round his feet.

"Yes, you've had a long journey, haven't you, Mr. Carlin? All the way across Europe and that took courage—lots of courage. Even though your actual escape was an accident, it showed courage. You had courage to get out from behind the Iron Curtain, courage not to give yourself up to the first Western cop you saw in Berlin, courage to come here.

"And I admire courage, you know. I admire it and I can always recognize it; possibly because I possess it to such a marked degree myself."

"Mr. Mott, you've had your fun." Peter's head slumped forward and he could no longer look at the man. "You asked for my story and you've had it. I've told the exact truth but I don't care if you believe or doubt me. Just do your duty. Phone the police and get it over."

"Phone the police! That would be extremely unwise, I should have thought." Mott's gingery eyebrows came up in a bar across his forehead.

"And not only unwise, but rather late in the day too. If you intended to give yourself up, you should have done so long ago; in Berlin, for example.

"As it is, why give yourself up now—when you've reached the very place you wanted to be, where the real work can start; the hunt for your wife's killer?"

"The hunt for her killer." With Mott's words, all tiredness had dropped away and hope was a little, ticking pulse in Peter's head.

"Just what do you mean?" he said. "Are you saying that you believe me, that you won't give me up to the police?"

"No, no. That's too fast, Mr. Carlin, far too fast. I'm not saying anything of the kind; not yet." Mott shook his head violently and frowned.

"All I'm saying is that I'm interested in your story. I also believe that you may not be a traitor. The fact that you're here and not still in Leningrad proves it—or seems to prove it.

"I know a little about the Russian intelligence organizations and they exist only on results. They heard something about this device your firm was planning and, when they found you were in Leningrad, and later received the Yard request for your repatriation, it would seem a heaven-sent chance to them.

"Whether or not you had the information would not

bother them. They would work on the theory you did have it and, if you were destroyed as a consequence, it would be just too bad. They would cover up their refusal to repatriate you by claiming you were a traitor who had fled to them to save his skin. This was done and our people swallowed it." Mott crossed the room and threw himself down before a big, Victorian writing desk. Somehow he looked rather like that desk; solid and ugly and quite indestructible.

"Yes, as far as treason is concerned, I am on your side. As to whether you are a killer, I'm not sure—not yet. My friend the commissioner gave me a sketch of the case against you and it's a very complete case, very complete indeed.

"However, the fact remains that you did come back from Russia, and I don't think you would have been stupid enough to commit such a crime, unless you intended to stay there." He looked up at Peter for a moment and then slowly shook his head.

"That's just my opinion though, and don't bank on the police believing it. Though, by and large, they are intelligent men, they go by facts, and facts alone. They like fingerprints and time factors and the testimony of reliable witnesses. And, in your case, they have all these things it seems; prints on the gun and in the car, which should have been parked at the airport, the statement of the maid that you left the flat together.

"Oh, they'll be sympathetic if you give yourself up. They'll congratulate you on getting out of Russia and they'll listen to what you say and search for fresh evidence. All the same, they go by facts, and if they don't find any—" He threw his hand across his throat and leered horribly.

"No, Mr. Carlin, we don't want to go to the police, not yet. First I want to satisfy myself as to your guilt or innocence. Then, we will do what we have to do." He leaned forward a little into the light as he spoke; an actor on the stage, the self-satisfied craftsman about to perform a task of which only he was capable.

84

"My friend, you have been very lucky. You escaped from Russia because a car crashed. You came right across Europe and found this crook in Berlin to help you. And now, now your luck has reached its climax. For I, Mr. Carlin—I am prepared to investigate this case of yours and help you."

Peter stared at Mott and his mind was reeling. The world had become just a dream and this man was part of it. He had not the slightest idea whether Mott was just a charlatan or what he exactly claimed, but he had to accept his assistance. He struggled for thanks but somehow the words would not come.

And Mott saved him any embarrassment. He raised his arm in the gesture of Mussolini silencing a Fascist mob and gave his repulsive smile.

"Yes, I know how you feel, Carlin, but don't thank me, not yet. At the moment, I am merely looking into your case for my own amusement, as an intellectual problem. One day you may thank me, but not just now. You see, if I find that you are indeed guilty, I shall hand you over to the first bobby on the beat.

"And now, having made my position clear, we will get down to business." He pulled open a drawer and laid a sheet of very thick, very white paper on the desk before him.

"Just now, Carlin, you gave me a general account of your career, your married life and your movements before boarding the plane to Russia. Assuming you have told me the truth, let's see how the real killer, or more probably killers, could have framed you so completely." He leaned forward and picked up a pen; somehow it looked ridiculous, a child's toy in his big hand.

"In the first place, he managed to make your wife's maid give a false statement. You say that this woman, Sommers, seemed loyal and devoted to her mistress, but, how much do we know about the human mind? What hate and bitterness and fear may be hidden beneath an always smiling face. Yes, all of us can be bought with the right threat or bribe, and Miss Sommers need be no exception.

"Fingerprints can't be bought though, and it seems this remarkable murderer was able to produce those too." He paused and made a note on the paper. From where he sat, Peter could see the writing. It was tiny and effeminate, with effected dots and strokes over the cramped letters. There seemed another side to Mott's character hidden in that stunted writing.

"Yes, fingerprints on the car you swear was parked at the airport. And, by the way, what was that car? Didn't you say you owned a Bentley?"

"Yes, I own a Bentley, or rather did own one. I didn't use it that night though. It was in the garage for a routine check-up. All that week, I'd been driving one of the firm's cars; a black Consul."

"I see, a firm's car, eh. A medium-sized, mass-produced car which, I presume, was fairly new and in good mechanical order. A car, which, to the driver, feels and handles exactly the same as a thousand others of its type and make. I expect you didn't even know its registration number, did you?" He watched Peter shake his head and made another note on the paper.

"And now, let's consider the knowledge of this murderer, for he knows a lot, doesn't he? He knows about your firm that you would call there on your way to the airport, that the watchman was old and idle, that you had planned a trip to Russia because of certain financial difficulties.

"He must have known about your home life as well. That your marriage had been on the rocks for some time. That there was a gun in the car. That your servant could be corrupted.

"And there is only one source from which he could have got all those things, one person who could have told him about them. And that is your wife. She, in fact, is the link between you and her killers. I use the plural because there seems such a lot of organization in this business; organization and power; fear and money." Mott's writing had changed now and his hand ran across the page in very quick shorthand.

"Therefore we shall start with the character of your wife and, through that, we will learn about her friends and her enemies and her movements; the things that made her tick.

"I've heard about the family, of course. A very proud, very old family, the Raynes. By all accounts, the father sounds a cross between a feudal baron and a modern saint. Yes, the papers called him that the other day, when he was opening some cripples' home. Sir Walter Rayne—the saint.

"Well, I suppose virtue and pride of race are good things, but only when backed by faith and achievement. When they come from nothing, except memories of the past, they go sour and rotten.

"And now, tell me about your wife, Carlin. You say that, about three months ago, something seemed to happen to her. You came home and found she had changed. How changed? Was it a breakdown, do you think? Some kind of hereditary taint that had forced itself through to the surface?"

"No, I'm not sure, but I don't think it was that." Peter thought, for a moment, and he just didn't know.

"I think something actually happened to her. Something she couldn't talk about because it was too bad or too frightening to repeat, even to me."

He lit a cigarette and tried to explain about Susan and the change that had come over her; the woman he'd married and the stranger he'd found in the flat when he came home. The stranger who went out alone and would never tell him where she had been. The girl who had grown old in a day and would never talk to him. . . .

"Please, Pete. Please don't ask me what's the matter. I promise that it doesn't concern you at all and I've done nothing wrong. No, I won't tell you." And finally, the head thrown back and the sudden flash of anger. "Oh, why can't you leave me alone?"

It was the first time he had fully discussed his married life with anybody, but, before Mott, it was oddly unembarrassing; just words in the confessional, the whisper from the psychiatrist's couch.

"And that brings me to the end of my story," he said at last. "To the reason I came back to this flat and risked being recognized. Susan kept a diary, you see. I was never allowed to look at it, but I saw her writing in it. And I think—just think—it might tell me the name of her killer."

He got up from his chair and stood in front of the fireplace. A cold fireplace now, because winter had turned to spring, but it still glowed with a life of its own.

The nymphs and shepherds still played below the mantelpiece, the carved vines and roses blossomed and the tall, Doric pillars gave it strength. A fireplace that only Grinling Gibbons could have made and which might just contain the name of a murderer.

"Yes, that's what I came back for, Mr. Mott, to find Susan's diary. It may tell us nothing of course, or the police have probably found it already. If they haven't though, if it's still here, I want to see it."

"Yes, quite interesting. A diary your wife kept during those last months, but which you were never allowed to read. No, the police didn't get it. I'm sure Winterton would have told me if they had. You're quite certain about this though? You know it existed?"

"I'm certain all right. I imagine it was a kind of safety valve to her. I saw her writing in it, you see. I also know she must have had a good hiding place." He gave Mott a small ashamed smile.

"Yes, I spied on my wife, Mr. Mott, and I often looked for her book."

"And you think it may be hidden in here?" Mott watched his fingers running across the carved walnut of the fireplace and then crossed beside him and stood frowning at the woodwork.

"You think this may have some secret drawer or sliding panel?"

88

"I don't know. All I'm sure is that the diary existed because, as I told you, I spied on Susan. It couldn't have been hidden in the furniture, which was modern, or the police would have found it. The floor is out as a hiding place too, because we had fitted carpets. That seems to leave this fireplace. It is a family heirloom which she brought with her and had installed when we took the flat. I seem to remember a story attached to it. One of her ancestors collected gems and used it as a safe."

"I see. Gems, eh. Precious stones and hidden papers and secret drawers. How very romantic; quite the *Boys' Own Paper*, in fact." Mott slipped off his coat and revealed a loud, chocolate-coloured shirt with scarlet stripes. The sleeves were pulled back by steel bands which seemed in danger of snapping against the thrust of his biceps.

"Well, secret drawer or not, we'd better check on it. It's ten to one that it isn't here and a hundred to one it will tell us nothing, if we find it. All the same, we'll make sure."

"Yes, we'll make sure." Peter knelt down under the mantelshelf and stared at the carving, searching for a crack that might betray the way in.

"It will take time though, I'm afraid. The man who designed this was a genius and, if there is a drawer or panel, they'll be well hidden."

"Will they, Mr. Carlin, will they indeed?" Mott scowled and flexed his muscles.

"It seems that you underrate my capacities, both mental and physical. If this thing contains a hiding place I intend to find it; and what's more to find it within ten minutes." He bent over Peter's shoulder, squinting at the wood and noting the run of the grain and the balance of its lines. Then, he crossed to the far wall and took something from it.

"Well, here goes. This may make my insurance company smart a little, but that's what the blighters are there for." The battle-axe he held was shafted by rhinoceros horn and terminated in a steel spike. Its cutting edge gleamed dully in the light and was a full foot across.

"Now, if you'll kindly step out of my way, we'll see if this piece of junk holds anything."

"Just a minute, Mr. Mott." Peter got up and stood in front of him. Even though the fireplace might hold his ticket to freedom and revenge, he revolted against the thought of its destruction.

"Before you use that axe, couldn't we try another way? Try to find the spring or lever which controls it? After all, this is genuine Grinling Gibbons and quite irreplaceable."

"Is it really? How very interesting. And have you the impertinence to suggest I am unaware of the fact?" Mott raised the axe and, for an instant, seemed about to bring it down on Peter's head.

"Well, Carlin, I have not the slightest idea of what value you place on your life, but my time is also irreplaceable. Now, get out of my way."

He bunched his muscles, swung the axe and a hoarse, bellowing roar burst from his lips. As the blade came down onto that delicate piece of furniture, Peter saw that Mott liked breaking things. His face shone with the joy of a Vandal amid the shrines, a Norse Berserker in the palace.

Eight times the axe fell, slicing through the mantel like cardboard, splintering the panels and shattering the carving below. Then he threw it away and looked at his handiwork.

And he had done his job well. There was nothing there now which could please the eye or delight the senses. There was just broken wood, fragments of inlay and the blackness of the chimney behind; ruin and destruction and rubbish.

All that and something else too—for lying amid the debris on the floor, was a catch, a metal spring and the thing the fireplace had died for. A little brown book lying open at his feet with Susan's story winking up at them.

Peter had read the book, as Mott had done, but it didn't make sense at first and told him just one thing; his wife was insane.

Who, in their right mind, could have written those disjointed sentences, and words which didn't hang together, and separated them with empty pages and aimless doodles, and, here and there, deep lines and gashes where the pencil had torn through the paper?

There was a great pain and bewilderment in his eyes as he looked at his wife's diary, and, then, slowly, the pieces started to hang together and he saw the sketch of a story.

For, though her mind was in agony, Susan had a story to tell. A story she had tried to conceal, even from herself; as though it were too bad, too frightening, to write down in a well-hidden book. Through that maze of disconnected writing, scribbles and fear, he saw a little of what had happened to her on that day, three months ago.

You get up one morning, and you're a happy, contented woman with just a few worries and none of them big ones. You have breakfast with your husband as usual, and you kiss him good-bye when he leaves for the office. Then, because you're a well-off, rather idle woman, you sit back over the breakfast things and wonder what you'll do with your day.

And it's a lovely morning for January. The street outside looks crisp and bright and there's a hint of spring in the air. So, you decide to go out and look at the shops. You always like doing that, even if you don't buy anything, and today should be no exception.

And, at the beginning, you do enjoy yourself—just at the beginning. After a time, you begin to feel ill-at-ease as though there is always someone behind you, watching your movements. From every shop window you look at, every counter you walk beside, there seems to be the reflection of eyes watching you.

But it's all nonsense of course, for who would want to follow you? It's just imagination and comes from one cocktail too many last night. You shrug off all thoughts of a watcher and go up to the store cafeteria for a cup of very strong, very black coffee. And, while you're drinking the coffee, the feeling of being watched becomes stronger than ever and you want to get up and run out. You can't though, because, at that moment, a chair is drawn back at your table, a voice excuses itself, and the owner of the eyes is sitting in front of you.

And, when you look at the owner of the eyes, you're not frightened any more, for it is a woman. A tall, gaunt woman in a costume which had seen better days a long time ago. A very ordinary woman that you'd hardly notice in a crowd; somebody's rather unattractive wife, somebody's mother, somebody's not too efficient secretary.

So, you smile at the woman who shares your table, and say "how noisy and crowded this place is becoming, and how nice the weather has been," and wait for some answering platitude.

The woman doesn't make one, however. She props up an old umbrella against the table, takes off her glasses and calls you by name. And, when she does that, the world starts to disintegrate.

Once, during the war, Peter saw a sailor fall in the drink. He was a very drunk sailor, and the drink was a dirty stretch of water between the wall of the Gladstone Dock at Liverpool and the side of a troopship called the *Maya Chieftain*. The sailor slipped off the gangway into the water and, as he was drunk and could swim, he didn't mind, but laughed and started to sing a bawdy song. Then, he stopped singing rather suddenly, because the ship moved a little and crushed off both his legs. Susan's eyes might have looked a little like that sailor's, as she listened to the woman in the café.

For perhaps a full minute, but it seems like a year, you sit and listen to a voice and hear your world tear apart. Then, without answering, you get up and walk to the phone booths at the end of the room. You fumble in your

92

bag for pennies, dial the number of the police, and very soon a bell rings and you hear them reply.

And suddenly you know you can't speak to them, that it is impossible to speak to them. You must know more first. You look through the glass door and see that woman sitting very confident and self-possessed and just beginning to eat a cream bun. So you put down the receiver and walk back to listen to what she has to tell you.

And, when she's had her say, you go out and walk the streets and try to think. But it's no use, for nothing makes sense any more and there's no hope and no solution.

All day you walk the streets and, when it's dark, you go home to your warm, cheerful flat, and the maid you've known since childhood, and your husband who will be coming home any minute.

But the flat seems cold and cheerless, and Ethel Sommers has become a stranger and, when your husband comes in, you can't talk to him. You want to of course. You want that terribly and you struggle for words which just won't come. And, all at once, you realize that it's no use, that there's nothing to say and not one person in the world you can talk to.

So you say you feel ill, but there's nothing to worry about and no need for a doctor, because you'll be all right in the morning, but it might be as well to sleep in the spare room. And, when you're alone, you take out your diary and try to write out what you feel.

And, in the morning, spring has lost its battle and it's January again. You listen to the rain on the windows and, for one wonderful moment, you think you've been asleep and the sound of the rain brought on a nightmare. Then, you feel the little book under the pillow and you know you've had no dream and everything has happened. You get up and go out and prepare to do exactly what the woman told you.

There was a long break in the narrative at this point and, for a few pages, Peter lost the thread. Then, almost at the end of the book, it came together again.

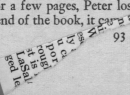

Susan had left the flat at about ten, and gone to the bank where she drew out all her housekeeping money. They kept separate accounts but, at a rough estimate, she must have had a little under three hundred pounds to hand.

When she came out of the bank, it had stopped raining. That was noted in the book as though it were somehow an important fact. She then walked to the nearest tube station and took a train. There were no details or name of the district she visited but the street was well described.

It was a short street, somewhere near the river, with tall, Victorian houses and a railway embankment behind. The houses must have been expensive once, but, with the coming of the railway, their original owners had moved away and they'd come down, through stages of tenement and slum, to warehouses, store-rooms and roofs over small, near-bankrupt businesses.

And Susan had been told to go to a certain public house at the end of that street. It was a little, green-painted pub which probably only carried a beer licence and its name was the "Harry Hotspur." She had recognized it at once by the sign of a man in chain-mail, swinging over the door.

She had walked towards the pub with her bag in her hand, and she must have been early. The woman had said they would meet in the private bar at eleven sharp but the woman wasn't there yet. She was coming down the street on the opposite pavement and she looked just the same as yesterday; tall and gaunt and shabby with the old, blue serge costume, the glasses and an umbrella which didn't seem to fold too well.

Susan stopped and watched the woman. She wasn't hurrying at all, but, at about fifty yards distant, she started to cross the road, not at right angles, but diagonally and without looking. She must have been about half way across when the car—

Once more the story broke off, as though Susan hadn't dared to write it down. Then it pulled together again and he could read clearly without fitting in the pieces.

"I've never seen death before," Susan wrote. "Only in

pictures and this didn't seem real. She was just there one second and then not there. Nothing that looked like a woman was there; just a thing like a doll, rolling and rolling down the street as though it wouldn't stop. I never imagined a body would go on moving like that. But, when I reached it, there were just rags in the gutter, covering something that didn't move at all.

"And I saw him too. Not his face of course, that was turned away from me but I saw his hand. Yes, I recognized that and, though it sounds ridiculous, he seemed to be smiling with it; smiling through the fingers as they held the wheel."

And that was almost the end of the story. Susan had watched the car round the bend and vanish, the crowd gather over the body, and then walked away. And she had gone on walking. All through the weeks and months she had walked across London, looking for something she had to find, but could never mention. Just on the last page of the diary, it seemed as if she did find it.

"I know everything now," she wrote. "I know the whole horrible story and tonight I'm going to talk about it. I have to do that or else go mad.

"And, when it all comes out, Peter will be in Russia I suppose. I wish I could have told him but, at the time, it seemed impossible. Now, it's all too late and I think he'd kill me for hiding it. Oh, my poor, poor Peter, what will you think of me?"

Peter closed the book and put it down. He had no idea what the story meant or what the woman had told Susan. It was too early to consider that yet. All he felt was a terrible sadness and despair at her words.

"Yes, interesting, isn't it? Very, very interesting indeed." Mott pushed away the notes he had been making and stood up.

"As I said to you just now, Carlin, everybody can be bought and all of us have a price. The opposite also seems to be true. I think that to each human being there may be something which is too bad to bear or even think about. It varies from person to person, of course. One of us may dread a death by drowning or impalement, for example. Another have a great fear of certain animals or insects. We rarely reveal these things, of course, even to ourselves, but they are there. And, if confronted with them, the mind withers.

"And your wife seems to have found her horror, doesn't she? She found it in the crowded cafeteria of a London store."

"Yes, she found it all right." Peter looked at the book, and for a moment, his fingers ran across the cover as though about to tear it apart. As though its mere destruction could wipe out the past.

"And it drove her mad, didn't it? This isn't the work of a normal person but Susan was sane, you know. Oh, I realize there is bad blood and bad heredity in every old family, but she was sane enough before this.

"And she couldn't even write it down, could she? She couldn't tell me and she couldn't even put it clearly in the book. She meets a woman in a café and that woman tells her something and tries to blackmail her. She goes to meet the woman the next morning and sees her killed—killed by a car driven by someone she recognized by a distinctive hand.

"Who was the woman and who killed her, Mr. Mott? What was the thing she told my wife that drove her insane?"

"I don't know yet, but, very soon, I intend to find out." Mott moved slowly across the room and stood frowning at him from the doorway.

"Yes, we'll find it, Carlin, and now I'm going to make a telephone call which might help us on our way. And, while I'm gone, I want you to think. I want you to try and remember anybody you've ever known who might answer the description of that car driver. Anybody who has something strange about the hand or fingers. The owner of a distinctive ring perhaps; the sufferer of a manual disease, scar or deformity. Think hard, Carlin, your life may depend on it." He turned on his heel and closed the door behind him.

But there was nobody who fitted, nobody at all. Peter racked his brains, considering every friend, relation or chance acquaintance, but there was nobody. After a time, he gave it up and, going to the window, pulled back the curtains.

It was quite late now and the lights of London merged together to form a red glow in the sky. Yes, it was getting on and, all over the enormous, sprawling town, the pubs would be emptying out. And, that would take time because it was Friday night, pay night, the start of the week end, and they would be full; the drunks hovering in the doorways, trying to sing, the waiters grabbing half-full glasses from reluctant leave-takers, the barman roaring "time" from behind his slopped counter.

In most of the pubs, that was. One or two would be almost empty, because they relied on the day-time trade and had no centre of population, no dwelling houses, to fill them by night. One called the "Harry Hotspur," for example, which stood in a street where the houses had died and become workshops and store-rooms and small, decayed offices. A street where a woman had rolled like a rag doll in the gutter.

"Well, Carlin, can you think of anybody who might answer that description, anybody at all?" Mott came back into the room and he carried a large pile of newspapers in his arms. He watched Peter shake his head and began to spread them out on the desk.

"I see. A pity, but it was probably too much to hope for. Well, while you've been thinking, I've been on the phone to Scotland Yard.

"Oh, no, don't be alarmed. I didn't tell them you were here, though that might have been a sensible idea, if the diary had read a little differently; had gone further to suggest your innocence. As it is, the last paragraph seems to put you back in the picture as the chief suspect. 'I think he'd kill me for hiding the truth.'

"No, I wanted to try and get some official account of the hit and run *accident* that killed the woman who was trying to blackmail your wife.

"The blighters were most unco-operative at first. They had the impertinence to ask what business of mine it was. Soon put them in their place of course. One mention of Tom Winterton and they started to crawl.

"Anyway, they promised to ring back as soon as they have the details. Shouldn't take long either; there can't be many bars of that name in London." He assumed the scowl which seemed to go with his more serious mental processes.

"And you're both a fortunate and an unfortunate man it seems, Carlin. Through great luck you manage to get out of Russia, but your wife did not trust you enough to give you her confidence. A maid you believed was loyal lied to hang you. And, then, a third person made a statement which was designed to bury you alive. No, no, please don't interrupt me yet."

He ignored Peter's question and started to rummage among the papers. He worked without care or order, throwing them impatiently to one side, like a bear hunting for food in a rubbish dump.

"Yes, there was a third person. A person who wanted to make sure that you would never be sent back from Leningrad to defend yourself." Mott had found what he wanted at last. His forehead creased with satisfaction and he grunted slightly as he read the news print.

"Just now, you told me you had no knowledge of the technical details of the circuit your partner designed. I was quite prepared to accept that statement. Why should an executive have such knowledge if his side of the business dealt with supply and sales?

"I wonder why the Russians didn't, though. On the whole they are a cautious people and, with their present policy, they wouldn't want to cause international hatred.

"They did cause it, however. They refused to repatriate a man wanted for murder. And, when they had you, they didn't bother to brain-wash you, or test your technical skill or even try to find out if you were telling the truth and were indeed ignorant. And, to the British demand for your return, they answered 'go to hell.'

"Now do you really think they would behave like that if they hadn't been so sure; do you think they would risk world hatred if they thought there was a chance you didn't know the circuit? Oh, no, they were sure all right, and so were our own people. They were quick enough to brand you as a traitor, because they were so sure." He leaned forward and handed Peter the newspaper. It was dated three weeks back and there was a picture beneath the headlines.

"They were sure, Carlin, for a very simple reason. Somebody told them."

The paper was torn and crumpled, the picture had never been a good likeness, but he could recognize it. Toni Marric stood before the door of their Number Two workshop, and he looked the same as he always did. The cigarette hung between his lips as usual, he stooped slightly, and the face gave no clue to his thoughts. Peter could imagine them.

He could imagine Toni standing there; being polite to the reporters, trying not to look bored or callous or indifferent and, all the time, longing for the moment when he could decently turn away and hurry back; back to his dusty drawing office, the figures on the table, the papers scattered about the floor, a slide-rule under his hand; his way of life.

He looked at the print below the photograph and its account of the transcribed interview. "Peter Carlin may have killed his wife," Toni Marric had said, "but no man could have had a better partner. I will always be grateful to him, whatever he did. We started this business on a shoestring and it was largely on his drive and initiative that it became a success."

And, though it was nice of Toni to have said that, it didn't mean a thing. For he had never known what that drive or initiative meant. He'd never even considered it, he'd just demanded the things we wanted.

"Pete, I must have a thousand feet of platinum wire!— Damn it, old man, you'll have to fob them off a bit longer. This thing must be exactly right before we start production."—"Well, go out and get the orders, because I must have two new Kretcher lathes."

No, Toni Marric had never known the work he'd done to keep them in business. The constant fight for orders and supplies and tools, while the dedicated scientist sat alone and bothered with nothing so trivial as cash or a finished product. He looked at the next column and, like a physical pain, he began to understand what Mott had said to him.

"Oh, no, Peter Carlin was not merely the business side of our partnership. Though he did little research himself, he was a fine engineer and, in a way, acted as second opinion to mine. Yes, he was familiar with all the firm's products. He would never let a job go through, without satisfying himself as to every technical detail."

And why had Toni said that? Why had he stood before those reporters and lied in his teeth? For it was a lie and he had never discussed a single technicality with Toni. He had always been the machine-minder of the team, the one who went out and brought home orders and materials. Toni would no more have discussed his beloved research with him than with the office boy. He let the paper slip from his hands and looked up at Mott.

"Yes," he said. "You're quite right. He told them and he lied. He knew it was a lie, so what was his motive? Why did he do it?" And, as he spoke he seemed to see Toni's hand on the wheel of a swerving car, and Susan writing in her diary, and Radek sitting before him. . . .

"Mr. Carlin," said Radek, from the past. "We know you can, so for your own sake, draw us that circuit."

And then, Radek faded and there was just Mott sitting frowning in front of him.

"We don't know yet," said Mott very quietly. "We've just started on the trail and, when we find that out, I think we'll be a long way home.

"Now, tell me about this Marric. We know he lied,

that he was a brilliant research worker, but, what else is there about him worth knowing? What was his background, for instance? What did his father do? What were his political sympathies? Tell me all you know about him in fact, and then, I'll try to tell you why he lied."

"Yes, I'll try." Peter searched for words to form a description, but somehow they wouldn't come. After one sentence, he knew that he had no picture of Toni Marric as a person. All he saw was a still figure bent over a mass of wires and tubes, a hand running across the drawing board and a voice saying, "I'm not sure yet, but this might work." Just a technical brain without emotion and feeling; nothing which added up to make a human being.

For Toni had no hobby, no sport, no girl, because he couldn't afford the time. He made good money, but lived in a single, furnished room in a house near to the factory. He seemed to have no views on religion, politics or art, and claimed not to have read a novel in fifteen years. Once, he had queued for an hour to see a new type of motion picture, and left after ten minutes when he understood the colour reproduction.

"No, I never really knew him," he said. "We met, by chance, after the war, discussed setting up in business together and pooled our resources. He was a brilliant engineer and a good partner, providing I kept a check on his more hare-brained schemes. That's all I can say about him. And, it may sound odd, but I don't really think there was much more to know. I think that he, quite literally, had no interest outside his work."

"I see, the dedicated scientist, eh. The single-track oddity who is in love with his job." Mott's fingers drummed quietly on the side of his desk.

"Now tell me something, Carlin. You said that, before your marriage, your business was in a strong position. Then, you neglected it, and it began to go down. It went down, because, left to himself, without you to hold him back, Mr. Marric was able to indulge freely in every brilliant but unprofitable scheme that came into his head. You see what I'm driving at, don't you?"

"Yes, I think I do." And as he thought, Peter seemed to see Toni standing before him. To see the sudden blaze of anger in his eyes as such a scheme had been rejected because it would cost too much to bring in too little.

Was that the truth? During all those years had necessary frustration led to hate? Was Toni Marric quite without emotion? Had he perhaps possessed a deep and abiding bitterness for all those ideas they had had to turn down?

And, all at once, he remembered something else. For it was Toni, the partner who took little interest in the financial running of the firm, who had suggested his trip to Russia. Left on his own he could have borrowed the money, from the bank perhaps, even from his father-in-law. But, for once, Toni had been adamant; the Russians had asked for office machinery, their "Calculator" was the best for its price, a visit to Leningrad was an easy and sure way out.

"Yes," he said, staring at Mott. "I think I understand. It looks as though, all the time, he hated me and at last that hatred came up to the surface."

"It looks like it." Mott's hand stopped drumming on the desk and he held it up to the light as though it were a rare and valuable object.

"And think of your wife for a moment. She is threatened with blackmail and prepares to pay up. She cannot tell you about this, which means that she is either deeply at fault herself or wishes to protect some person she loves or is indebted to.

"Then the blackmailer is killed by a car which fails to stop and she recognizes the driver by his hand. And we've thought about that hand, haven't we? We suggested that, to be recognized, it must have had some marked physical characteristic; a deformity perhaps, a scar or a ring.

"Maybe we were wrong. Perhaps it was quite an ordinary hand but still recognizable to someone who knew it very well; to a lover perhaps." Mott looked at the sudden tightening of Peter's face and went on.

102

"And, after the murder, your wife goes through real agony. For some reason she cannot fully reveal the truth; even to herself. I wonder, however, if, just at the end, her conscience became too strong for her, and she did decide to talk. And, so, the killer planned another murder; a very clever murder this time, because the chief suspect would never be able to defend himself. No, he would be safely buried in Leningrad at the orders of a man called Radek."

He broke off and, as he watched Peter's face, he knew that he had gone too far, for the man was starting to crack. Peter had come home, not merely to save himself; it was hate and the need for revenge that kept him going; the dream of the beloved wife and the hope of finding her killer. Let that dream die; let him see her, not as the pure, shining girl but an adulteress, and he was finished.

"Easy, son," he said and there was something very like compassion in his big, arrogant face. "Just take it easy and remember that I said *perhaps*. We know nothing yet, and my theory is just pure supposition.

"And this might tell us a little more."

The phone rang in the next room and he got up from the desk and went to answer it. For a full five minutes he was gone, and when he came back, his voice was very low and thoughtful.

"Yes, your wife tried to disguise the story, but she gave us the facts and they tie together. The 'Harry Hotspur' is in Stepney at the corner of Silver Street and Mark Lane. On January the eighteenth, a woman, named Molly Pleyden, was killed outside it by a car which failed to stop.

"And, though there were no witnesses to the actual killing, a porter from one of the warehouses saw the car. He couldn't take the number but he described the make and year. Yes, it was a black Ford Consul, the same type of car you drove to the airport; the same as that in which your wife died." He sat down and scribbled a note on his sheet of paper.

"The woman will interest you too, I think. She was

described as a widow, but it's her maiden name that concerns us. It was Sommers. That's right, Molly Sommers and, I imagine, the sister of a certain loyal maid who lied to hang you."

It was really night now and most of the town had gone to bed.

Peter lay very still on the top floor of the one-night hotel, where Mott had sent him in case the police paid a surprise visit to the flat, and for the first time in weeks he slept soundly.

He had walked very quickly to that hotel and all the time he had sensed a follower. It was a male follower he feared though; a man in a trench-coat, a man in uniform, a plain clothes policeman. Twice he had looked behind him, but when he saw there was nobody of that description in the street, he had gone on. He had gone on and never noticed the middle-aged woman in a faded, blue coat who drifted so aimlessly after him.

But now he slept and, in his sleep, he saw the face of Susan, and behind it, another face which was made up of Mott and Toni and Gregor Radek, mainly of Radek. From every angle of his dream the face of Radek seemed to be looking at him.

Apart from that, he slept soundly and, around him, tired commercial travellers, clerks and bookies' runners slept too.

And, in the Kensington flat, Moldon Mott was asleep. He slept on his back, stretched out on a camp bed, and, from time to time, he snored and muttered in his sleep. At the foot of the bed, a silent, razor-billed sentinel, the bird, Wellington, kept watch.

But, less than a mile from Mott, there was a man who couldn't sleep, because he had been interrupted. The man lay on a big bed with a canopy over it and he listened to the telephone in his hand and looked at his room.

He liked that room very much, for it seemed to reflect his own personality; a florid, self-confident man in a room full of plush and gold and heavy furniture. There was a bulge on the bed beside him, but the woman who made it had left when the phone rang and the man was quite alone.

The lamp on his bedside table lit up the walls of the room and, all around him, the heroes of the Revolution scowled down from their frames of gilt and carved plaster; Lenin before the Kronstadt sailors, Voroshilov working his gun at Tsaritsin, the mutineers on the battleship *Orel*. As he listened to the phone, he looked at those pictures and wondered if, one day, he would stand among them.

"Yes, naturally, I am sure," he said at last and there was no expression at all on his face. His face didn't need expression, for it was the face of a technician; the mask of an expert who did his job supremely well.

"The man, Carlin, reached England this morning and he has been followed since leaving Dover.

"What was that you said?" His mask of a face didn't alter but there was suddenly a little, ticking pulse of anger above the left eye.

"No, I will not arrange to kill him for you. I want no scandal here and I have no murder organization at my disposal. Yes, perhaps it would be better if you came yourself, I think. Your department got us into this mess and you will get us out of it. Yes, my dear colleague, I am glad you understand me. Carlin must die, but you—and you alone—will be responsible."

He replaced the phone and picked up a book beside him. The book had a very bright cover and its author was Miss Agatha Christie. Poytr Kun, head of Soviet Intelligence in Britain, was a great reader of detective stories.

CHAPTER SEVEN

BACKWARDS and forwards, deep in thought, Mr. Mott paced the floor of his den. Had he considered at all, he would have thought he resembled some grave captain, alone and commanding upon the bridge of his ship. To a possible observer, however, his attitude might have seemed nearer to the frustrated march of a caged ape.

He was thinking about two stories. One was the purely domestic and sordid tale of blackmail and murder, and the other reached out into the fields of international politics. And the link between those stories was made up of lies.

So many people had lied; a maid whose sister was killed by a car which didn't stop, a wife who couldn't tell the truth till it was too late, a scientist who made a false statement to bury his partner alive.

Yes, so many lies, and so many characters. Since early that morning he had considered them, but not one fitted together or seemed to connect. For he no longer believed in the theory that Susan had been Toni Marric's lover. It was too pat, too easy, and the woman who wrote that diary had not been merely anxious to protect some one, but terrified. The truth, when he found it, would be something much more horrible.

Not that he had any doubts he would find the truth. His self-confidence was boundless, just let him gather a few more facts, and he would move in and the matter would be finished. He took one more walk across the room, pushed the diary into his pocket, and marched out to find those facts.

It was a lovely day and, as he stepped out onto the

pavement, he felt like a Colossus, a Hercules ready for battle, the "Good Giant," as the French had called Conan Doyle; for, either way, he had to win.

If he satisfied himself that Peter Carlin was guilty, he would hand him over to the police and glory would be his. If, however, he could prove his innocence, then, how much more praise would there be. His big, gingery face creased into a smile and his moustache curled upwards as he thought about it; the struggle of a giant against the world; the one man who had faith and the genius to support it; the hero who succeeded when all others had failed.

He imagined the old, authoritative men talking together in clubs. "Yes, that's Mott. J. Moldon Mott, the feller who solved the Carlin case. Brilliant piece of work and he's sure to get a mention in the next Honours list."

And, he damned well would get a mention too. It should have happened years ago but petty jealousies had stopped him. This time no one would dare to stand in his way. His mind started to ring with resounding titles— "Sir James Moldon Mott"—"Lord Mott"—"Baron Mott of the Amazon."

And he was almost sure now that Peter was innocent. There was still a lot against him of course, *too* much to risk contacting the police, but it was, in a way, *too* much. It was all too contrived and Peter's return from Russia and their discovery of the diary stood in his favour.

But, if Peter were indeed innocent, then they were not up against any single killer but a very large and powerful organization. He was quite sure of that but it didn't distress him in the least. He would break that organization. He would break it in the face of the whole world.

His car was parked on the opposite side of the road, and he growled a hymn as he walked towards it. Though the tune lost flavour in his deep, toneless voice, faith and belief were there and the words came out loud and clear to the amazement of passers-by.

"For we whose steps are lighted by wisdom from on high—Shall we to men benighted, the lamp of truth

deny?" sang Mr. Mott and, flinging open the car door, climbed into the driving seat.

He didn't start off at once, however, but leaned over the back and picked up a canvas bag which his garage had put there. There were two things in the bag and they had taken a lot of explanation to have made. One was a simple screw clamp which he attached carefully to the gear stick, and the other was a steering wheel. There were spring clips fixed to it and they slid over the original wheel to hold it in position. He grinned as that false wheel snapped home and twirled it gently with his hand. When he saw it was firm, he knew one of the means by which Peter Carlin might have been framed.

Then he started the engine, moved the gear lever with his clamp and drove off.

He went out of London through the western suburbs and he drove badly, without care or consideration for other users of the road. His hand was always ready on the horn behind a nervous driver and he cut sharply in front of lorries, cursing back at their occupants with verve and pleasure. In front of fast traffic, though, he showed a marked tendency to hug the crown of the road.

And the car reflected his type of driving; a big, heavy car that carried the scars of its owner's personality. The paint was chipped and scratched, there was a ragged gash down one mudguard and the front fender hung loose and twisted. The power was there, though, and in less than half an hour he stopped before his destination.

The factory which Peter Carlin had built stood back from the main road in a cul-de-sac and, already it had been altered. There was a big, hanging sign over the gate which was blank and shiny with new paint. Recently it would have read "Carlin and Marric," but that was finished now. "Carlin" was no longer a good trade slogan and it was dead and done with and best forgotten; the name of a man who had done something unspeakable and vanished from decent knowledge.

For a long time, Mott sat in his car and looked at that factory. Though it was Saturday, half day, he didn't hurry. He removed the clamp and the false wheel, lit a cigarette and waited; the spy in the camp, the tiger at the gates, the first of the invaders waiting to enter the "open" city.

There was a lorry unloading inside the entrance and, from the line of saw-tooth sheds, he heard a whirr of machinery. Then a bell started to ring, the machines stopped and the now-empty lorry drove away to the back. It was the moment he had been waiting for; Saturday noon, the end of the week, and, already an army of work people were beginning to come through the gate.

The young men came first. They came quickly and purposefully, as though their tools had been flung aside at the first peal of the bell, and the football queue had to be beaten. They hurried past him towards the bus stop, and the car park and a few, a very few, carried straight on towards the big public house on the corner.

Then came the women and they were in groups, laughing and chattering together, and, one or two, painting their lips and powdering their faces, as they hurried on to freedom. Like the young men, some made for the buses, some for the car park, and some for the pub.

And, at last, heavy and ponderous, came the tramp of the main force, the élite corps, the old guard, the people who made the factory tick. Between fifty and sixty, most of them, but they all looked alike, whatever their age or colouring or build; cloth caps at exactly the same angle, the same slow, unhurried tread, the same, slightly pompous expression on their faces; the faces of the skilled working class, the seven-year trained artisan, the craftsman who knew his job and his value.

Mott watched them march stolidly past him, a lot more making for the public house than the other two groups, and then, he looked back at the gates. Apart from a few stragglers, they were empty now. Apparently the office staff either worked later hours or shunned that crowded exit. He got out of the car and followed the stragglers into the pub.

It was comfortably crowded in the bar; comfortable

and warm and happy; because the week end had begun, there were notes in each pocket, the lathes and drills and presses had stopped, and there were just football matches to be watched, gardens to be dug and a long lie-a-bed in the morning. The atmosphere was just beginning to thicken with pipe and cigarette smoke and, from the end of the counter, a group of women laughed shrilly.

Mott stood in the doorway for a moment, and his bulk almost filled it. He watched the crowd and was gratified to see one or two of them turn and stare at him and a slight hush fall over the laughter and conversation. Then, he walked to the counter and ordered a large brandy.

"Thank you, landlord," he said as it was put before him. "A lovely, lovely day, is it not? And, if I may make so bold, you seem to have a very lovely clientele." He leered horribly at the group of women and raised his hat. At the same instant, he somehow managed to wink at the men around him.

And it worked, as he knew it would. If the factory had been anywhere else, they would have considered him an outsider acting in the worst possible taste. In the North or the Midlands he would have been greeted with sullen stares from the men and a haughty tossing of the heads from the women. But he was on the outskirts of London, and the Londoner loves an eccentric. Besides, to most women, there is a strange fascination in a really rude and ugly man and Mott was both these things. There was a roar of laughter, a chorus of welcoming giggles, and he had broken the ice.

He made the most of it, lolling back against the counter, and taking more than his fair share of room, but he paid well in entertainment value. He discussed football and film stars, God and the "telly" and told an unprintable and quite untrue story of the private habits of a certain politician. And, when the ice was really broken, he drew away from the crowd a little and began to single out a possible informant.

Her name was Kate, and she was a big woman; big and

strong and coppery, like Britannia on a coin and just the type Mott liked. He didn't draw back, as the press of the crowd forced them together, but leaned forward feeling the thrust of her breasts through the overalls and smelling her odour; a good, healthy odour too, which almost made him forget the job in hand.

Almost, but not quite, for, although, at the moment, merely a pleasant bar companion, it seemed that Kate Robbins was a person of some importance in the factory. One of the first employees to be taken on, and now a fore woman in the machine shop. Just the kind of person who could tell him the things he wanted to know. He joked with her, flirted with her, watched innumerable Guinness stouts vanish down her handsome throat and finally got down to business.

He took his time about it of course. These people had had their fill of reporters and questions about the Carlin case, so, very gradually he led the conversation towards it. It didn't take too many glasses of Guinness to get Kate's views.

And to his employees at least, Peter Carlin had been a popular figure. He had worked hard, was a good organizer and always seemed helpful and friendly. "Strange to think of him doing a 'orrible thing like that."

Susan too, they had liked. In the old days, she had often visited the works and created a good impression on everybody. The women had liked her clothes, and the men her smile and sway of her body.

Yes, the Carlins had been well thought-of in the firm of "Carlin & Marric."

But they didn't like Toni Marric. They didn't like him because they'd never known him. To them, he was a mystery, a man who worked alone and seemed to look right through them and never spoke except to make demands. A man who sat alone after hours and, when he came out, was a hurrying shadow walking away without a word of greeting. Kate's voice hardened as she spoke of him.

111

"Something nasty about a chap like that—something uncanny. Gives me the creeps every time I look at him."

But, however much they'd liked the Carlins or disliked Marric, there was no doubt in their minds as to Peter's guilt. The facts were clear, the case was finished and there was nothing more to be said about it. He'd killed his wife, in a fit of temper or insanity, and fled to avoid the consequences.

For it stood to reason really. "He'd worked a screw loose," shot her in the car, and got out quick. And, in his head was the knowledge which could bargain for safety.

Of course he'd known about the circuit. Everybody in the firm knew Marric was working on something special and he and Carlin must have discussed the details together. Why, Marric had said so himself to the newspaper men, hadn't he?

And Carlin and Marric were the only ones who did know, because Marric was close and didn't even talk much to his draughtsmen. All they ever saw were separate bits and pieces. The complete drawings were kept in a ruddy great safe in his office.

Yes, perhaps Carlin did seem a nice chap, but it must have been an act. After all, what do we really know about people, when it comes down to it? At the end, he'd shown himself in his true colours. A bastard who killed his wife and then sold his country to the Russians.

And, as Mott listened to her, and watched her face, and looked along that crowded bar, he knew she was speaking for all of them. There was not one person in that crowded room who doubted Peter's guilt.

He started to change the conversation then. He turned it away from Peter, and the things Peter was said to have done, and talked about Kate's job and how the factory was run. He was very interested in that because, all at once, he knew he had to get inside that factory. He wanted to get inside it, and sense its atmosphere, and learn all he could about it. For he was almost certain that it was there and not in any Kensington flat that Susan's murder had been planned.

112

And he played his cards well. "Rather an ignorant chap in some ways," he said, hating the falsehood. "Spent most of me life in the bush or on the veldt—never seen the inside of a modern machine shop—wonder if it might be possible to have a look round?"

It was possible and there was an odd ache in Kate's big body as she looked at him, for she thought Mott a fine man. A fine, strong man who could show a girl a thing or two. She liked the way he talked, and the way he listened, and the way his great, gingery moustache curved upwards when he grinned. With the Guinness a warm glow inside her, she felt she could have done anything for him.

And it was nice of him to want to see where she worked. A form of compliment; for an important person like this Mr. Mott couldn't really be interested in a little tin-pot workshop. He knew how to treat a woman all right. Not like some she could think of who were this minute queueing up to watch twenty-two hirelings kick a football about.

Yes, it would be very nice to show him around; make her feel important in a way. Old Welford, the watchman, would let them in, and they wouldn't be too long about it. Just a quick whip round and then back to the bar for a couple before closing time. And after that —who knows. There was a nice piece of steak in the fridge back home, and Mr. Mott might be persuaded to share it. She drained her glass, nodded to the barman, and walked out.

And Mott strutted and smiled as he followed her. Things were going well and he would be able to inspect the factory at leisure with an excellent guide. Already he fancied he knew a great deal about Susan Carlin's murder.

But there was one thing he did not know, and he might have walked with a little less self-confidence, had he foreseen it.

The thing was Death, and in a very few minutes, he would quite possibly be burned alive.

113

Peter Carlin walked out of St. Paul's Station and looked around him. Behind stood the gigantic loom of the cathedral, and, in front, he could just make out the tall cross of the Central Criminal Court.

Peter had spent the night in the small, incurious Bayswater Hotel, as Mott had told him, and, all day, he had wandered across London. It was foolish of him perhaps, but he had to do it; even at the risk of being recognized. He had sat in the cafeteria, where the woman had first approached Susan, and he had drunk in the "Harry Hotspur," where she had died. A useless pilgrimage which had to be made; as though the mere sight of bricks and stones could give him a lead to his wife's story.

And now, he was going to meet Mott. There was a card in his pocket which read "Parbat & Refique—Importers and Exporters" and gave an address at Frenten Street in the City. Mott had told him to go there after tight and, if there was any luck left, Mott might have learnt something by now.

Though it was still early, the City of London slept. All around it, from the docks to the South and North and the bright streets of the West, the sky was a throbbing red glow, but its own sky was dark; a dark, lifeless sky, covering the tall buildings with their barred doors, the closed shops and empty, ill-lit streets. It was like a town that had lost a war, been evacuated and now waited for the invaders to march in.

And, with Monday, those invaders would come. With morning, they would assemble at a thousand suburban out-posts and the attack would start. Then, the Army of Occupation would pour into the City from buses and tubes and crawling Wateroo railway they called the "Drain." Then, the streets would fill with their uniforms of black and grey, the doors would open, and the banks and counting houses and insurance offices would come alive again.

But not yet; now it was the week end and the City was alone with its dreams of ships and gold and ten percent

114

and mergers of the past. Now it was closed up and didn't want the tiny men and women who served it. It didn't want a single, living thing; even the cats who patrolled its empty street seemed interlopers.

Peter walked on, out of the station towards the river, and, suddenly, he felt the hostility of the City. He felt more alone than he'd ever felt in Russia or Berlin, for, there, his enemies were obvious and he'd known what he was up against. Here, among these dark, empty buildings, it was quite different. Here, every doorway could hold an enemy whom he would never know till the knife flashed, a gun exploded or a hand came down on his shoulder.

For the enemies must be after him by now. Quiet men and women would have spoken together and, in a quiet room, somebody's hand would have drawn a cross on the map and somebody's voice said—"Look there." He had no illusions about Radek or the organization that Radek served. From the time he had limped out of the Berlin underground, they would have sorted the evidence, marshalled their forces and started to move in. They couldn't be very far behind by now.

And, soon, his own people would know he was back; if they didn't know it already. Somebody in a train, in a street, in the hotel foyer might have looked at him, wondered about him, and then gone to the police. At this very moment, the constable standing below the lamp at the end of the street might hold his description in his pocket.

And Susan's killers would want to find him too. Mott was quite definite that there were more than one and, for all the man's vanity, he was beginning to trust him, for Mott was his one link with the outside world, his one chance of learning the truth.

But how many were his enemies, how lonely was the quiet City, and how loud were his steps on the pavement. As he went on, the words of Macbeth seemed to run through his head—"*Hear not my steps which way they walk, for fear the very stones prate of my whereabouts.*"

115

Yes, his feet were suddenly like drums on the concrete rising to crescendo and telling the world where he was. He fought back the desire to run and, turning up his collar against the few spots of driving rain, walked on towards Frenten Street.

Behind him, far behind and taking it slow and easy, as though there were no need to hurry, a middle-aged woman in a faded blue coat followed.

And, all at once, he seemed to be out of the City and walking through country. Suddenly there was grass beneath his feet and no more buildings, but bushes and small trees around him. Here, they had cleared the bombed ruins but not yet started to build, and nature had taken over again. The sycamore seeds had floated across the broken cellars and taken root, the grass had spread between them and, where there had once been blackened bricks, there was earth and rank plants and, here and there, a fair-sized tree. To his left, an owl hooted three times, and, in front, he could see the staring eyes of a rabbit. His own eyes were full of envy as he watched it turn and vanish down some safe, warm hole in the ground.

Then he was through the wilderness and back into town; a line of tall, lightless buildings, a plaque marked "Frenten Street" and number thirty-two almost straight in front of him. He hurried across the street and up a flight of steps leading to the place where Mott had promised to meet him.

The door opened at a touch and the hall within smelt of old linoleum, cats and pine disinfectant. Beneath his feet, the floor creaked loudly as though even the boards were in conspiracy to betray him. There was no light, but, in the flare of a match, he could read the varnished information board with "Parbat & Refique" on the top line and an arrow pointing upwards. He blew out the match, pushed the spent stub back in the box, and started to climb the stairs.

And, on the next floor there was another sign and another arrow. The paint was chipped and scarred this time

116

and the lettering had obviously been done by an amateur. Whoever they were, "Parbat & Refique" seemed to be in a small way of business.

He went on, following the arrow, with the lino giving way to bare wood and the boards creaking still louder as though in danger of collapse, and, at last he was there; standing at the top of the house on a little, narrow landing, with heating space to the right and a frosted glass door labelled "Parbat & Refique" in front of him. He was beginning to think he would remember those names.

But the room behind the door was obviously empty. In the dim glow from the street he could make out two desks with phone and typewriter, a shelf of books and a steel filing-cabinet by the window. There was no sign of life and it was just a small office shut and closed for the week end.

No, whoever they were, whatever their business, Parbat & Refique were not expecting him. He was quite alone in that house and, after a time, he began to curse Mott for keeping him there. And slowly annoyance changed to something much more definite. Fear.

For, after all, what did he know about Mott? He knew he was a traveller, an explorer, a writer of adventure stories, but what else? How did Mott live, for example, and who paid for those expensive expeditions? And why was he so ready to help a murderer on the run? Was it merely from interest and a desire to prove himself more efficient than the police, or for quite another reason?

Why had Mott happened to take that one flat out of the whole of London? Was it just because it was vacant, his friend, the commissioner, had helped with the lease, and it suited his needs?

Perhaps, but only perhaps; could it have been for none of these things but for quite a different reason? Could he have been paid to take it; paid to sit like a spider in the web and wait for Peter to return if he ever got back from Berlin?

If he got back. And why *if?* Perhaps Mott had known

all the time that he was on his way back; had known of the car crash beyond Pushkin Village, the secret-police passport opening the frontiers for him, and the man reeling backwards in the Berlin station; had known the whole story.

And, if that was the case, there was no need to wonder who Mott was, or who paid him for those journeys across the world. He could put a name to that paymaster and see his face. The face of a man who sat in an office behind the "Oulitza" and was very fond of animals; the face of Gregor Radek.

And he, Peter Carlin, had done exactly what Radek wanted. He had fallen for the oldest confidence trick on earth and had accepted help from a man he did not know. He had taken the bait, hook, line and sinker, and now they had him. They had him just where they wanted; on the top floor of a deserted office building, with no watchman, no passers-by, to hear the things they did to him.

They were coming too. Even as the thoughts ran through his head, he heard them. The door had opened below, there was a groan of floorboards, and footsteps were coming up the stairs; heavy, heavy footsteps coming slowly up the stairs to fetch him.

But they weren't Mott's footsteps. He could have recognized those, for, even with the man's bulk, there was a jaunty springiness about them. These steps were slow and dead, as though belonging to a cripple or someone carrying a burden. Mott had played his part as the decoy and moved out of the story; now the executioner would be taking over.

He looked wildly round for a means of escape, but a second's glance told him there was none. There was just the office in front of him and its window ended in a three-storey drop. The only way out was to try the impossible; to face those feet on the stairs and try, just try, to fight his way past them. He crouched at the end of the landing and waited.

And they were almost there now; heavy and leaden and slow, coming up with a lot of purpose behind them. He braced against the stair-rail, saw a shadow begin to grow on the wall and, behind the shadow, came a dark, hunched shape carrying something that gleamed.

He counted three slowly, arched his body and sprang. He almost reached that dark shape, when a thing like a windmill caught him, picked him up and carried him downwards.

CHAPTER EIGHT

He came down those stairs like a tree falling; slowly at first, and then in a gathering rush, with wood splintering around him, and the breath beaten out, and a weight which was steel wrapped in cotton-wool holding his body and forcing him down.

He lay on the second landing with a light coming on, and his arms pinned by the weight above them, and fingers reaching for his throat. Lean brown fingers on his throat; fingers as slim as a girl's kneading into it. And he couldn't get at those fingers for the cotton-wool weight that held him. All he could do was to look up at the face above his and see death in it, as the knife came out, hovered for a moment, and started to go home quickly.

And suddenly it was finished. As though on a spring, the face was jerked backwards, the knife fell away and the weight left him. Then he was pulled to his feet and another face was before him. A face, dark and bloated with fury, was scowling at him and a voice shouting words which were slurred and run-together.

"And what, Mr. Carlin, is the meaning of this—this outrage?" Mr. Mott pushed him roughly back against the wall and stood beside him breathing deeply. His expression was a mixture of anger, hurt dignity and complete astonishment.

Peter didn't answer for a moment; he couldn't. His breath wouldn't come at once and there was fire in his throat cutting off speech. He looked down at the floor and saw the thing that had held him beneath the knife;

120

a big, padded divan bed with one leg hanging broken and loose and a long tear down the upholstery.

And, behind the bed, a man was standing; a thin, slight man with a lean, brown face, a beard and a great deal of hatred in his golden eyes. He bent down to pick up the knife again and his expression showed how much he would like to use it.

"Yes, Devi, you may well look annoyed, but I think, in this case, we are dealing more with a fool than a knave." Mott still scowled but there were beginnings of humour in his face. Tucked under his left arm was a pink bed-spread and a pillow.

"Yes, Mr. Carlin has been under rather undue strain during the past weeks and we must humour him. When we were a little late, I imagine he felt he had been led into some kind of trap and became desirous to escape. That is so, isn't it?" He listened to Peter's stammered explanation and then turned on him like a blight.

"I see. So you thought I was some kind of a spy, did you? Some sort of Bolshevik agent? How stupid can a human being become? I have spent the whole day working on your behalf and then, because I was a little late, you let the most insolent and ridiculous notions get the better of you." He took a handkerchief from his pocket and blew his nose violently as though to drive home his feelings.

"I was late, Mr. Carlin, because I wished to make you comfortable. It is not safe for you to stay long in hotels and this will be an excellent hiding place. Mr. Parbat and I were bringing you a bed. We were carrying it up to the office when you made this vicious and unprovoked attack on us.

"And now, having got that off my chest, I'd better make the introductions. This is Mr. Devi Parbat, my very good friend and your present host."

"I'm sorry, really terribly sorry." Peter went forward to the small man and held out his hand. "There is no excuse I can offer except panic, but please forgive me."

For a moment, the man didn't move. His eyes still

121

glowed with hatred and the stiffness of his mouth made the knife look very sharp and near. Then, suddenly, his face relaxed into a smile and the knife was pushed away.

"No forgiveness necessary," he said. "Bona fide error and quite forgotten." His hand took Peter's and pumped it up and down.

"Devi Parbat at your service. Once assistant to Mr. Mott—once Serang on the steamship *Alcoma*—at present, businessman; importer of jute and tea, also brass ware and carpets. Very happy to help and conceal any friend of Mr. Mott's."

He bent down and swung the bed onto his shoulder. It was big and heavy but he made it appear to weigh nothing.

"I have been many years with Mr. Mott; both in the Hindu Kush and in Africa, Mr. Carlin. Saved his life on two—no, three occasions. Once he fell into a glacier and I pulled him out with a rope no thicker than my little finger. Another time—"

"And that is quite enough of that, Devi Parbat." Mott frowned and tucked the pillow more firmly under his arm.

"Neither Mr. Carlin or myself have the time or inclination to waste on boastful, personal reminiscences." He turned on his heel and marched up the stairs. The bedclothes he carried looked light as feathers and, behind him, the little Indian seemed hidden under the divan.

"And you've seen my partner?" Peter sat on a bentwood chair looking at Mott, while Devi Parbat fiddled over a gas ring making tea.

"Yes, I've seen Mr. Anthony Marric; rather more than seen him in fact. Ah, thank you, Parbat." Mott accepted a cup of near scalding, almost back liquid and sipped it with an expression of utter disgust.

"I'll tell you of our meeting in a minute, but first I want to go back over some ground. Last night, you told me that it was on Marric's suggestion you went to Russia to raise this capital your firm needed. Now, apart from the advantage of opening a new market for your calculating machines, was that really necessary? Couldn't you have borrowed the money quite easily; from your father-in-law perhaps?"

"I suppose so, but I'm not sure, not really sure." As Peter thought, a picture came into his head. A picture of old, mellow buildings and rolling lawns; buildings which needed a fortune to preserve them, and an old man bent over papers which were appeals for charity; so much for the polio hospital, so much for prisoners' aid, so much for cancer research; Sir Walter Rayne, the man they called a saint.

"I don't honestly know," he said. "If he'd had the money I could have borrowed from him, but I never knew what his finances were. He is probably a rich man, but that house of his, 'Steynnings,' must have taken some keeping up. He'd never consent to open it to the public and it may well have cost him every penny he had."

"I see. So your partner could well have been right. It may have been necessary for you to go to Russia and raise money to save a near bankrupt business. Always assuming of course that your business really did need money to save it." Mott put down his cup and smiled at the query in Peter's eyes; the wide, self-satisfied grin of someone who has done a job to his entire, personal satisfaction.

"Yes, it might once have been necessary for you to go to Russia, but not now; certainly not now. You see, Carlin, at this moment, your firm has no need of money at all. It stinks of money."

For there was money in that factory, lots of money. He saw it as soon as he came through the doors. New machines stood on the benches, and many of them had makers' stickers still attached. Foreign machines mostly, German and Italian, ordered and supplied from stock, much, much quicker than an English firm could have done. According to Kate Robbins the first batch had been delivered a fortnight ago, and more were expected next week.

Yes, there was money there. Money which had come

in very soon after Susan Carlin died, money which might just have been the payment for Mr. Marric's false statement to the press and the police. The statement which had given him complete control of the factory, and left his partner to rot in Russia. Mott thought a good deal about that statement as he walked through those rows of new, silent machines. All the marks of freshly-found prosperity.

And there was one machine that was not silent. It was a big, metal tank, twelve foot square perhaps and about eight feet deep. A low humming noise came from concealed gas jets around it, and a chute led up from its mouth to a ramp above.

He questioned Kate as to its function, and learned that the thing was a molten salt bath and used for the heat treatment of light metals. The temperature inside the tank was a constant five hundred degrees centigrade and, after immersion, a piece of metal would remain soft and pliable for a full two hours. Out of pure curiosity, he climbed into the ramp and looked down the chute.

And there was something horrible about that expanse of liquid salt. For though five times above boiling point, it was quite still and no heat seemed to come from it; as though it held the heat, ready and waiting for a victim. He thought of tales of acid baths and quick-lime, and knew they were nothing compared to this. A body falling down that chute would wither as the first grain of salt touched it. He looked up from that still, grey sea, and saw Kate wave frantically at him. Then he turned and knew he was not alone on the ramp.

Toni Marric stood six feet away from him, and he looked quite different from the newspaper photograph. That had just given an outline of his features, recognizable, but not adding up to a personality; and the person behind that photograph was quite removed from what Mott had expected. He thought of Marric as the comic-book scientist, the absent-minded professor, the egghead with uncut hair and thick glasses. This was one of the most handsome men he'd ever seen and he had three faces.

Yes, he had three faces which added together to make Adonis, and the first of them was Italian. There was all the joy of the sun in that face, and laughter which he'd lost but never quite forgotten.

And the Italian was the least important of his faces, and the second was Irish. A face full of gay cynicism that came from despair, and memories of empty villages and untilled fields, and all the things that Kathleen had cried about. All the things that the Saxon had done; the burnings and the closed churches and Cromwell's horsemen riding to Drogheda. All the past acts that would never be forgotten or forgiven.

And over both those faces, was the one that mattered. It was neither gay nor cynical, because it had done with emotion, and there was just one thing that held it together: curiosity. The compulsive desire to know why "A" differed from "B", why such a piece of metal fused and another remained constant.

"Who are you, and what are you doing here?" Marric's voice was flat and toneless as a self-recorded gramophone record. The kind of record you made before the war by dropping a coin into the machine and speaking slowly before a microphone. It was a voice that might have belonged to anyone. And, as Mott listened to it, he knew that at least part of his early theory was wrong. This man could never have been Susan Carlin's lover.

No, Toni Marric couldn't have been anybody's lover. For there was no warmth in him, no desire in him, which would bring him to a woman. He'd finished with the flesh years ago, and his lust was only for patterns; patterns of glass and metal and plastic, the way to send a rocket home.

And looking at him, Mott saw quite clearly why Kate and the other women in the factory had hated this man. It was merely because of his appearance. If he'd only looked as he should have done, the stereotype of a scientist, they might have forgiven his indifference. But they'd never forgive Toni Marric with his face of Adonis looking through them as through shadows on a wall. No. Marric might be capable of both murder and perjury, but not for love, not for anything as trivial as a woman.

"Good afternoon, sir," he said, taking off his hat and bowing slightly.

"Your charming employee here offered to show me round the factory. Though not an engineer myself, I am most interested in the subject and hope it is not inconvenient."

"No, it is not inconvenient. It is expressly forbidden." Marric turned away from him and looked at Kate.

And, as he turned, Mott saw something in his face he had not noticed before. It came from the structure of the eyes and the way they focused, or failed to focus. A pair of good, brown eyes flickering slightly in the sunlight that came through the glass roof. A flicker which was no nervous tick but spread over his whole face. A slow, weary movement like a clock which needed winding and was about to run down.

"Yes, Miss Robbins," he said. "It is forbidden for any strangers to be brought into this building without my permission. Just as it is forbidden for any employee to return here after working hours. And you know that perfectly well, Miss Robbins." Marric took a scrap of paper from his pocket and made a note on it.

"Yes, you have broken my regulations and you are discharged. Return here on Monday to pick up your cards and any money that may be owing to you. Now, get out."

And the fury in that dead, metallic voice took Mott off his guard for a moment. He didn't start to storm or protest or say what he thought of Marric, he just stood and watched. And, as he watched, he realized something else. Kate Robbins did not merely dislike this man, she was terrified of him.

She had brought him into the factory because she

126

thought Marric would have left with the others, and the drink had given her confidence. Now all courage from alcohol had gone and her big body seemed to shrink. She was a strong, capable woman and he would have expected her to argue or answer back at least, but she didn't. She just turned and walked away with her head down; an oddly pathetic figure among the rows of gleaming machines.

"And you, sir, I know you." Marric swung round at Mott and his words seemed to burst out as though someone else was speaking through him.

"Yes, I know you and your type. You've come here to spy, haven't you? To spy and watch me and check on my movements. You're one of two things; a policeman or a reporter and I've had enough of you. For three weeks I've been haunted by you, ever since my partner killed his wife and stole my invention. But this time it's gone too far. This time you're getting nothing out of me." His hands twisted together as he spoke, and Mott noticed something about them that might tie up with the story. They were blotched and discoloured by stains and acid burns and they might have been recognized on the wheel of a car.

Yes, Toni Marric was a potential suspect all right. His hands were distinctive, he had something to hide and he was terrified. It was terror that had made him sack the woman and turn on Mott the way he did. All the same, though Marric might be guilty of perjury to make the factory his own, though he might be a killer, he was not the one they wanted; the prime-mover who had planned Susan's death like a military operation. This man with his marked hands and twitching face was just a pawn in the hands of somebody else; somebody much more cool, and much more powerful.

So Mott tried to play him. He leaned forward on the ramp before Toni Marric and he cursed him. He cursed him and derided him as a nervous, guilty fool, and an unjust master who had just sacked an employee without cause. He hurled every insult he could think of at him, in the hope that he might crack. In the hope that he would lose his head and give a lead to the person or persons he served.

But suddenly he stopped. He broke off in the middle of his tirade and stared at Marric's face, and, all at once, he knew that he'd gone too far, and death was very close to him.

And he should have known it before, should have realized what he was dealing with, should have read the signs in those flickering eyes, and the sweat running down the forehead, and the body that couldn't keep still. For, though Toni Marric was half Italian, half Irish and English born, he was also the citizen of another kingdom. A wide, free kingdom whose subjects were of every race and creed and whose frontier was the world; the great Kingdom of Cocaine.

And, as he looked at Marric's face, a passage he had once read long ago came to mind. "The alcoholic will lie and steal and cheat but rarely goes further. The drug addict when provoked however, is always a potential killer."

Yes, Toni Marric was a cocaine addict, and he, Mott had gone too far and was very close to death. Marric's hands no longer twisted together for one of them rested on a lever at his side. And it was quite clear what that lever was. It was the control to the hydraulic mechanism which operated the tank behind him. Let that blotched hand move slightly and the guard to the chute would draw back, the ramp he stood on would tilt forward and he would go down. Go down with his hands clawing at nothing to a bath of molten salt five times the temperature of boiling water.

Mott stood quite still, watching the drugged fury on Marric's face, seeing him fight to control his hand, and he felt no fear, but a great anger.

For his conceit was such that terror of death was a stranger to him. Though completely agnostic where the rest of humanity was concerned, he had a deep and abiding faith in his own immortality. If he were to die he firmly believed that he would rush straight to paradise; the honoured guest of a benevolent deity who bore a strong resemblance to himself.

No, he wasn't frightened of death, of its manner; nor yet it seemed possible that he, J. Moldon Mott, should end his days at the hands of a man like Marric, a cocaine addict who wouldn't kill for reason or hate but merely because he couldn't control his body.

Incidents from history ran through his head as he stood on that ramp. Stories of the great and powerful being brought down by small contemptible things; William of Orange breaking his neck on a mole-hill, the Norman Conqueror brained by a falling beam, Marat dead in his bath—no, not Marat. The man was a minor figure, unworthy of comparison. Tamburlaine perhaps. Yes, he felt sure some mean, petty trick had brought Tamburlaine down.

He was very, very close to death, and there were just two alternatives open to him. Marric's conscious mind might not wish to kill him, but Marric was possessed by dope and anger, and his hand lay on the lever. If Mott stood quite still, the anger might pass, but it might also grow and become action. If, on the other hand, Mott were to move, what would the reaction be?

He thought for a moment, watching that crazed, drugged face, hearing the roar of the gas jets behind him and smelling the salt. Then he made up his mind. He started to walk forward along the hinged ramp.

"And you made it, Sahib, he did not dare to injure you?" Mr. Parbat leaned forward, and patted Mott on the shoulder. Though full of good feeling, it was a small, nervous pat. The action of a child with a large dog.

"Of course he didn't, and don't ask damned silly questions. I would hardly be here if he'd pulled that lever." Mott scowled and finished his cup of tea.

"No, Mr. Marric seemed to come to his senses when I

129

walked towards him. He just turned and almost ran away from me. I think he must have gone back to his office, but I didn't bother to follow him."

"I see. And you're sure he was doped, you're sure it was cocaine?" Peter's mind was full of bewilderment as he listened to Mott's story, for the person he described was not the Marric he knew. That Toni Marric neither smoked or drank and the thought of stimulants was repellent to him.

"Oh, yes I'm sure about that all right, and I've seen the symptoms before. He was far gone in addiction, though the habit may have been fairly recent.

"Yes, somebody has been feeding Mr. Marric dope, and that person is the one we want. You see, though Marric lied and was paid for lying, though his hand is distinctive, though, with the drug inside him, he is a potential killer, I don't believe he murdered your wife or the woman Sommers. No, we're a little nearer the truth now, but we'll have to go a long way before we reach the end of the story."

"But who? Who would have wanted to kill Susan, who needed to frame me?" Peter racked his brain for an answer, but there seemed nobody—nobody at all.

"I've no idea, Mr. Carlin, not yet. But I can see a possible solution, thouh it's still vague and probably untenable. As I said before, this business points to not one single killer but an organization, a very unpleasant organization indeed." Mott leaned back and closed his eyes for a moment, as though trying to marshal his thoughts.

"I don't want to go into that now, as it's a horrible possibility, and I hope I'm wrong. One thing I have found out today though, and that is the practical side of how you may have been framed; the evidence of the car and the gun which is supposed to have killed your wife."

He told Peter of his experiment with the false steering wheel that morning, and, as he listened, Peter saw how it might have been done. A black Consul outside the flat, which he thought was his own, but wasn't. For his own

130

had been removed and it was another Ford that waited for him. And as one mass produced car feels very like another, he'd never noticed the exchange but driven it to the airport. And, round the corner, his own car, fitted with a wheel cover to preserve the fingerprints, was ready and waiting to take Susan to her death.

Yes, it could have been like that, and, if so, the gun might have been the same. His gun fired once, held by wire or thin pliers, to leave no marks, and another gun killing Susan. A gun fired through her head against an open car window, so that the bullet would pass out and be lost forever.

"I see," he said. "Yes, it could have been that way." And though Mott's experiment was helping to prove his innocence, he got no comfort from it. Only dread of the methodical mind that had killed his wife, and planned everything as carefully as a military operation.

"And what's the next move? Where do we go from here?"

"*We* don't go anywhere, Carlin. You are going to stay here. Though the killers may not know you are back in England, the Russians probably do, and our own people as well. You will remain here and sweat it out, while I use my brains, and Mr. Parbat employs his talents in a little blackmail." He scowled at the Indian's faint gesture of protest.

"Oh, yes you will, Parbat, and I rather doubt if it will be the first occasion. You see, Mr. Marric lied and he was paid to. He was paid both in money and the complete control of your factory. Well, there is another person who lied, and she may have been paid as well. That's right, Miss Ethel Sommers, the loyal and devoted maid who states you left the flat with your wife at nine o'clock.

"For it seems that Miss Sommers has gone up in the world of late. I've traced her address, and tomorrow Mr. Parbat is going to call on her. And, if he plays his cards

131

well, I think Miss Sommers may crack, and you'll be a free man."

In a musty, over-heated room at the back of Whitehall, a man wearing evening dress was turning a file. The man's name was Colonel Salter, and he was in an even fouler temper than usual. This time he had some excuse for it. An urgent telephone message had interrupted his preparations for a dinner engagement, and brought him round to his office.

Yet, as he turned the pages, the ill-humour on his face gave way to interest, for he was an official of Her Britannic Majesty's Intelligence Service, and his job was his first love. What he read seemed rather more attractive than the Savoy Grill menu.

"Yes, strange isn't it," he muttered to his assistant. "Strange and rather fascinating. This fellow, Carlin, kills his wife, and hooks it to Russia with a possible military secret. Now he is said to have returned home.

"Not that there's a lot of evidence however. A customs officer at Dover thinks he recognized Carlin travelling under the name of one George Henderson, an American citizen. He doesn't report it at the time, but after looking at Carlin's photograph in the press, becomes more certain. God damn these imbeciles who have hunches and confirm them later." The good colonel knocked his pipe out on the floor. The thought of somebody else having to sweep up the ash made him feel a little better.

"Well, that may not mean a thing, but we check up with our people in Berlin where this Henderson is said to be living. And, from them, we learn that Henderson never came to England at all. He is still in the suburb of Charlottenburg, engaged in manufacturing synthetic sausage skins." Salter threw the papers to one side, and began to scribble a note on his pad.

"And it's all impossible of course, it has to be impossible. Carlin is an almost proven murderer and a probable traitor who fled to Russia to save his skin. He won't come home to face the music. Why the hell should he?" He tore the sheet from his pad and handed it to the rather crushed girl who stood beside him.

"Let the news agencies have this anyway. It can't do any harm, and if there is any truth in the idea that Carlin came back, it might bring him in. He's no professional crook with a score of friends to help him, but just one man on his own. He has to eat and sleep and travel, and the chances are he'll be spotted.

"And that's my lot for the night." Salter got up, tucked the white scarf into his coat and hurried out. He was only ten minutes overdue, the Savoy was a stone's throw away, and he would be able to sit down to dinner in good time.

He had done his duty as a soldier should, and the thought that it might well kill a man would not have worried him in the slightest.

CHAPTER NINE

MISS ETHEL SOMMERS sat in the front parlour of *her* rented, furnished, but soon to be paid-for house, and poured whisky from *her* bottle into *her* glass.

And the word *Miss* was important to her, though still strange; one more symbol of a new life and self-respect. For there would be no more *Ethel* now, no more *Sommers*, without handle or title. They had died with Susan Carlin weeks ago, and there was Miss Sommers sitting free and her own mistress, among the bricks and furnishings that would soon belong to her.

Yes, it was all so strange. Strange to sit on chintz, in a room facing South, and put your feet up if you wanted to; strange to go to bed when you felt like it, and get up in your own good time; strange to know that, if a bell rang, it would be your phone or your own front door, and nobody was going to give you an order or tell you to pass on a message.

Yes, three generations of domestic service, forty years of tidying rooms for other people to sit in, making beds for other people to lie on, and cooking meals for other people to eat, made it all seem very strange.

She drank deeply and greedily from her nearly full glass and looked at the phone beside her—*her* phone. She had chosen it specially, and it was exactly the same as the one that had stood by Miss Susan's bed; scarlet and cream with a little, plated band round the mouthpiece. She liked that phone very much and longed for it to ring.

"Yes," she would say, taking her time to answer and speaking very coldly. "Yes, this is Miss Sommers and what can I do for you?" That would be a pleasant change from the drilled formulas of the past. "Sir Walter Rayne's residence"—"Mr. Carlin's flat"—"Yes, madam, Mrs. Carlin's maid speaking, may I take a message?"

Yes, the phone too was another symbol of freedom; freedom from answering bells, taking orders and waiting at table. Pleasantly given orders it was true, but still orders—still to be obeyed. "Just run down to the post for me, Ethel"—"Lay another place for dinner to-night"— "Be an angel and iron this dress."

Yes, a whole life spent waiting for orders and looking after other people's comfort, as your mother and grandmother had done. A whole life wanting to change your job but somehow never managing, because change came hard to your nature and you feared it.

All your life sitting in a kitchen and knowing how dull and drab it was, and how crabbed and bitter you were becoming and loathing it; till a bright, well-rested voice with money behind it spoke to you and said—"Oh, Ethel, how stupid of me. I should have told you to go to bed hours ago." And you had to listen to that voice, and thank it, and try to warp your tired face into a grateful smile.

But it was all past now, and her life had paid off in the end. She'd taken the lot her background had told her to take, but now she was free; free in a little warm house of her own, with five thousand pounds in the bank and a weekly allowance paid regularly. It had better be paid or she'd have an interesting story to tell. Her thin, bitter face creased into a grin and she slopped more whisky into the glass.

But Sister Molly hadn't accepted her lot. Molly had played it smart, or tried too play it. Walked out of the house at eighteen, Molly had, with a smirk on her painted face, and no notice given, and "no more washing your dirty dishes"; to a job in a factory, a career on the stage and, at last, the trot, trot, trot down Wardour Street, till she was too worn and rotten for it.

Yes, Molly had tried to play it smart, and where had it got her? Four pounds ten in her purse, twenty times that in debts, and death in the gutter from a car which didn't even bother to stop.

She'd played it smart; but it was the elder sister, the meek one, the one who accepted fate and obeyed orders, who came out on top in the end; five thousand quid to her credit, a nice house and regular payments for a few, little lies.

And, after all, they were just little lies; though she felt sorry for poor Miss Susan. Miss Susan had gone to pieces, as so many of the Rayne family had done in the past. She'd seen it coming for months in that white frightened face, the trembling hands, and eyes that wanted to weep but never could.

Carlin had seen it coming too, of course. He'd watched the mind starting to crack and, one night, he'd lost his temper and killed her.

Yes, that was how it was. He left the house at nine but then rang back and asked Miss Susan to meet him. She couldn't be really sure, of course, as Miss Susan had answered the phone herself, but it must have been like that. She'd always disliked Carlin and was quite certain he was the killer.

Yes, Carlin did it. The letters said so and she trusted the writer of those letters; for he'd kept his bargain so far. A home of one's own, freedom, security and the future, for one little lie—one false statement to the police; "They quarrelled, made it up, and left the flat together at nine o'clock."

Yes, that was what she had been paid to say, but it didn't really matter for Carlin had killed her. He'd fled to Russia, hadn't he, which proved he was guilty. Carlin was a traitor, as well as a murderer, and she hated him for that. As present householder, ex-domestic servant, she feared communism more than any Tory squire.

But all the time, as she sat in that warm, cleaned-for-herself parlour, fear and guilt were very close to her and even the whisky could not really shut them out. She'd drunk a lot of whisky that afternoon and her feet dragged a little on the carpet, as the door bell rang and she went through the hall to claim the expected installment of her reward.

And it wasn't there, as it should have been. The day was Sunday, the time six-thirty, and payment was due. She should have seen a thick, brown envelope lying on the mat and heard the sound of anonymous footsteps walking quickly away before she could look at their owner. She frowned, pulled open the door and stood staring at the man on the steps; a little dark man, wearing a turban, with a basket under his arm.

And, looking at the man she was suddenly reminded of the words from the past. "Who is it at the door, Ethel?" "Oh, nobody, madam, just an Indian pedlar. I'll send him away."

But Miss Susan hadn't let her send him away. She felt sorry for him, and asked him in, and gave him coffee, and even bought some of his trashy goods. Yes, the mistress of the house had talked for an hour with that pedlar.

Well, she, Ethel Sommers was the mistress of this house, and she'd ask a pedlar in too, if she felt like it. Not that she felt sorry for him of course. He was just a wretched parasite on society who ought to be doing a proper job. She'd make him no coffee either, and she certainly wouldn't buy any of his shoddy rubbish. It might give her pleasure to waste his time though; to watch him unpacking all his goods and then send him off without a farthing.

"Come through," she said curtly. "I don't like standing on the doorstep. Mind you wipe your feet though."

"Thank you, madam, thank you very much indeed." Devi Parbat lowered his basket and bowed deeply while his dark eyes studied her.

He saw a tall woman whose breath smelt of whisky and whose face was without love; completely without it. Her eyes could search for ever and see nothing but cold, hostile people in every corner of the world.

He followed her through the passage into an overheated, chintzy living room, and he noted the way her steps dragged slightly, and felt the sour atmosphere of the house closing in on him. It was an atmosphere which came from cooking, and spilled drink, and unopened windows, and another smell which he had heard about years ago. There was a name for it in his own country, and they said it was made up of envy and fear and the nearness of death.

Yes, he recognized the smell, and, though Miss Sommers looked quite strong and healthy, it told him she was soon to die.

But that was not his business. He had come to gain information, to play the simple, cringing pedlar, till the right moment came and a certain question could light up the fear in her eyes. He knelt down, opened his basket and began to whine out the virtues of his cheap scarves, export-reject stockings, and table mats.

And Miss Sommers enjoyed herself. She leaned back like a queen, with the whisky glass in her hand, and sneered at his goods. She liked doing that very much.

"No, no, not that," she said. "Show me something else —something better, if you have it. Yes, pull it all out and if there is anything worth taking I'll buy it. Oh, dear! Have you nothing else but rubbish?" There was almost lust in her face as she looked at the small, bent figure cringing before her.

But, when the last article had been laid out, mocked and derided, it seemed that Parbat still had something to sell. He pushed the goods back into his basket, stood up and smiled at her; the warm, begging smile of a dog watching a banquet.

"Give me money, Memsahib," he said. "Even though you buy nothing, please give me money. You see, I am such a poor man and I have to walk the streets all day, and sometimes all night too. And, when I am walking, I notice things—very interesting things too, on occasion. Give me a little money, Miss Sommers, and I will tell you about one of those things that I saw."

"You know my name? You've come here to beg? Why, you—" She started with surprise and annoyance, and, though she managed to break it off in time, Parbat

ensed that the word "Wog" had been on her lips. Some-
now, that made his task a little less distasteful.

"Yes, Memsahib Sommers, I know your name and I
think I can be of service to you—great service." He
watched her face and his own was no longer meek and
humble but full of threat.

"You see, one night, not so very long ago, I am outside
a block of flats in Gloucester Road. I think of going into
the flats, but the porter seems an angry man, so I begin to
walk away. Then, a man, a nice, rich-looking man comes
out of the entrance, and I think of going up to him and
asking for the price of a drink.

"The man is in a hurry though. He gets into the car
and drives off, before I can speak to him. I remember
his face however. Yes, I remember it very well. And, a
few days later I see it in a newspaper. I read that paper
very carefully, Miss Sommers, and I start to wonder. I
wonder why a certain lady told a lie. Why did she say that
this man left with his wife, when he was alone; when I
saw that he was alone?

"And that is why I started to look for you, Memsahib
Sommers. I want your advice, you see. I want you to tell
me what I should do. Should I go to the police and say
what I saw, or would it be better if I kept quiet? Would
it be more profitable for me to keep quiet, Miss Sommers?"

It worked. The hint of blackmail was going home,
as Mott said it would, bang in the centre of the target.
The woman's head drew back, her hand shook, spilling
whisky onto the floor, and there was suddenly fear in her
eyes.

Yes, fear was there, and more than fear, much more;
stark terror. And that wasn't what he'd expected. He'd
expected rage and anxiety and furious denial, but not
this. Not this complete collapse, with the mouth wide
open showing the blackness behind, the twitching hand,
and the wide eyes which seemed to be looking past
him.

And, suddenly, he knew the truth; she was looking

139

past him. Her eyes were staring at the door behind him and in each pupil he could see a reflection. Ethel Sommers might be terrified, but not of him. He, with his false story and puny threats, meant nothing to her now. It was the thing behind him that mattered.

For there was someone behind him. Someone who had opened the front door, while they were talking, and came as quietly as a cat through the hall. Someone who was by his back now, for he could feel breath on his neck and hear the beat of a heart which was not his own. He stood quite still and waited for that person to move.

And, when it came, the explosion was not the important thing. It was so close that heat blast fanned his hair and his ear drums seemed to split open, but he hardly noticed it. All he noticed were the woman's eyes, for she had three of them. Two pale eyes still carrying the reflection behind him, and a third exactly in the centre of her forehead. Yes, a single, red eye turning black, as she reeled sideways, knocking the telephone to the floor, splintering the glass in her hand, and falling at his feet: just a bundle of rubbish that looked as though it had never lived. And, as she fell, he heard a voice.

"Turn round," said the voice behind him. "Turn round very slowly and carefully and look at me. Ah, thank you, that is much better." It was a soft, purring voice, very used to giving orders.

But Parbat never saw the face of the owner. All he saw was a hand. A hand which was oddly deformed, holding a gun he could recognize—Webley, .45 calibre—British Officer's Standard Pattern—First World War Issue. A gun that looked as heavy and archaic as a Frontier Colt. He had dealt in arms in his time and there was almost professional interest on his face as he looked at it.

And then the big gun spoke again, and its blast seemed to push him down very gently, till he lay beside the dead woman on the carpet. And there was strangely no pain at all. Only numbness at first and something that felt like warm water running down his back. Then feet moved towards him and those deformed fingers were reaching for his pulse.

And, with those fingers, memory came and knowledge. For though Parbat was now a dealer, a merchant, one who bought cheap to sell dear, he had once been something else, and he hadn't quite forgotten his training.

As the fingers reached for his pulse, he seemed to see an old, wise face before a shrine, and hear a voice repeating wisdom that came from no text book.

"It is sometimes possible to look on death," the voice had said, "and the way is by concentration on nothingness, on the negation of all matter; the loss and complete denial of personality."

And, as he remembered those words, the earth seemed to become a void, the wetness on his back stopped, and, for perhaps three seconds, his heart was still.

Then, the fingers left his pulse, as though satisfied, there was a sound of cloth rubbing metal, and, like the most precious gift in the world, the big gun was pushed into his hand. He smiled slightly as the fingers wrapped his palm around it, and there was joy in that smile. A great, great joy, for he would not be going out without revenge it seemed. Let those feet draw back a little more, and he and Miss Sommers would have a companion for the long journey.

But when the feet did draw back, he suddenly knew it was no use, for he couldn't move the gun or start to lift it. It had been put there to prove him a murderer and a suicide, and would probably remain just that; for it had become heavy, terribly heavy. A lead weight, clamped to the floor, which he could never move in a hundred years. And, behind him, quiet and easy, as though satisfied with a job well done, those cat-like feet walked out of the room, and his hope of revenge died.

No, there would be no revenge for him, but there might, just might be something else. By his hand lay the telephone which had been Miss Sommers' pride. The scarlet telephone which was beginning to blend with the growing stains on the carpet.

Very slowly his hand crept towards that telephone and his fingers started to turn the dial. They turned with difficulty, as though turning an enormous weight but, in time, he heard a bell ring, and a voice he knew answer him.

"Sahib, listen to me," he said. And pain had come now and every word was fire in his mouth.

"Sahib, I have failed you. Yes, as the English say, 'I have made a ruddy balls of it,' so listen carefully."

For a full minute he whispered into that scarlet phone and, when he stopped, he never heard Mott's reply. All he heard was a distant noise, that might have been the wind through trees, but was his own blood seeping into the carpet.

And, soon, he didn't even hear that. He had been a long time a-dying, but he was dead at last.

And, a little time before Parbat died, Peter Carlin saw fate close in on him and knew he was finished.

Mott had left him that morning in the Frenten Street office with the promise to return by nightfall and dire warnings to stay put.

He'd tried to obey Mott. He had to obey him because Mott was his sole ally now, his one contact with the outside world, and he trusted him. There was so much confidence in Mott, so much strength and energy, that he felt, by nightfall they might be a long way home.

Besides he had to stay put. All over the town his enemies would be closing in and the Frenten Street office, which nobody seemed to use, was at least a hiding place. He was out of the battle now, and all he could do was to sit back and wait for the others to carry on the fight.

And he did try to. All day he sat in that bare room making tea, longing for a proper drink, and trying to sort out the wild thoughts that ran through his head. And, at last, he drew back the curtains, opened the window and looked out.

It was getting dark early that night. Dark and cold with a trace of fog drifting up from the river, the street lamps haloed, and a clock striking the hour from the cathedral. It was striking seven and he counted each note carefully. And, on the last note, he leaned out a little farther and saw Fate look up at him.

Fate lay in the gutter, lit up by the nearest street lamp and, though it was three stories below and quite small, he recognized it. And, as he recognized it, Mott's warnings became unimportant and meaningless, and he went out of the office and down the stairs to meet it.

The newspaper was sodden and discoloured, but of that day's date and it told him he was finished, for a picture was on the front page. Not a good likeness perhaps, and taken some years back, but still easily recognizable. His own face looking up at him and headlines above it—THIS MAN COME BACK?

Yes, that sodden, discarded paper in the gutter told him the truth. He was finished at last and the chase was over. He had come a long way to revenge Susan, and, at every turn, he had found friends and allies to help him. He had come through the Iron Curtain and across Europe, but it was all over now. He was home, his own people knew he was home, and he couldn't hide and run from the world any more. Suddenly nothing seemed important to him except the thought of a drink. He needed that like an alcoholic in his final horror, a drowning sailor searching for a spar to hold him up. With one last glance at the paper, he walked away down the street.

The bar stood on the corner and it was dimly lighted, almost empty and a bored barmaid hardly glanced up from her knitting, as she put the whisky before him. He drank it in one gulp, ordered another and then moved to the back of the room to consider his position.

When he had read that paper and walked down the street he had already made up his mind. He was going to give himself up. When he had finished his drink, he would go to the police and tell his story and pray that

143

they would find fresh evidence. If he did that, there was no need for Mott or Parbat to be brought in, and nobody but himself would suffer.

But with the whisky courage began to return. False courage, possibly, just Dutch courage, but still there, warm and glowing, and in it there was the core of an idea.

For, though he had no time left, perhaps he didn't need it. Perhaps there was still a way to the truth and a quick way. It was a hundred to one against it working, of course, but he had to take it; a way through the fear of Toni Marric.

For Toni Marric was frightened, frightened to death. Toni Marric had lied to bury him in Russia, and Toni must at least know part of the story. Let him just get Toni alone, and he might see the face of the person who killed his wife.

Yes, that could be it; that could be the way out. For there was no time for any other, no alternative. Toni would be sitting at home now; sitting and dreaming of his new machines, and new authority, and the freedom to plan and design exactly what he wanted.

Well, Toni Marric's dreams would be interrupted. The corpse he had helped to bury was out of the grave and coming to its loyal partner for help. "Yes, Toni, I'm back. Never mind how, but just help me. You've got to help me, because we're partners and you're the only person I can turn to."

And, if he played his cards it might work. If Toni thought he was without suspicion, he might meet him, might do anything to stop him going to the police. And, in a quiet place, he would drag the truth from Toni, if it were the last thing he did.

Yes, that was the way. The only way left, because the sands had run out and there was no more time. A single phone call, a stolen car driving down to Reigate, and a quiet meeting in the one place that seemed fitting; in the empty cottage where Susan's body had lain. The whisky on his empty stomach and the chaos of his mind made that action seem good.

144

They also hid from him the fact that he would very probably die that evening. For, if Toni Marric swallowed the bait, if he came to the place of meeting, would he come alone? As Mott had said, Toni was no prime mover, but just a pawn. And the people who were his masters, the people who had killed Susan, might well come with him.

No, Peter didn't think of any of those things. He just looked round the almost deserted bar and prepared for his first move.

And the first move was to hand. The phone stood on a shelf beside him and it had a coin box, but no partition. The fact that it was open to public view didn't trouble him in the slightest. He pressed in his pennies, dialled the number and waited. After a moment's pause he heard Toni's voice; a faint, sad voice that might have been speaking from the end of the earth.

When he replied to Toni, he spoke in German. It was just a small precaution and he felt it was probably unnecessary. The only person within earshot was a middle-aged woman in a faded blue coat and a worried air, who looked as though she were completely taken up with her glass of stout and a great many private troubles; bills and debts and an unpaid mortgage, and "if only my husband could get a better job." He ignored her and concentrated on his story.

And, after five minutes, he knew that the first part of the scheme was working. Toni Marric would meet him and Toni Marric was terrified. That faint, sad voice seemed to come from someone he had never known. Someone who had seen the Gates of Hell open and would agree to almost anything. Peter put down the receiver, and, almost with hope in his eyes walked out of the room to prepare for that meeting.

And, just as soon as the door closed behind him, the woman got up too and took his place at the phone. She was such an ordinary woman, so very English looking, that a chance listener might have thought her words odd had he heard them. Like Peter, she spoke in a foreign language, but the language was Russian.

Peter didn't look for a car just at once, he had something to do first. He had to go back to the Frenten Street office and leave a note thanking Mott and Parbat for all their help and kindness. He didn't want their help anymore, but he would mean what he said—really mean it. They and Judah Schlot and Lottie Steiner and the cripple on the Berlin train had tried to help him, and he would never forget that till his dying day. He smiled slightly as he thought of the phrase; *his dying day*, that might be very soon now.

But, it seemed that he wouldn't have to write a note after all. The light on the landing was burning, though he remembered switching it off, and the glass door was open, though he remembered locking it. While he was out, somebody had come into that office; somebody who was sitting at the desk and breathing deeply; heavy laboured breathing with a hint of sobs in it, as though struggling for air. He crept across the landing and peered through the gap between door and lintel.

Mott sat at the desk with his head in his hands and the ruin around him was extraordinary. The filing cabinet was on one side, burst open like cardboard, a typewriter had been hurled against the wall, and, everywhere, the room was scattered with books and papers and broken office machinery.

Very slowly he looked up at Peter and he didn't seem to recognize him at first. His big face looked dazed and bewildered and, when he spoke, the words were slurred and quite lacked their usual bombast.

"I killed him," he said in that strange, old man's voice. "I sent my friend to his death because I made a mistake, I didn't realize what kind of people we were up against, you see; and, because of that Parbat died. He died with one last wish; the wish to tell me what he knew." Mott got up from the desk and walked towards Peter. Though his body still looked massive and brutal, it sagged and some of the strength seemed to have left it.

146

"Parbat was almost my best friend, you know. We'd been together so often in the past; the Hindu Kush, the Amazon, and many, many times in Africa. And, at last, when he'd saved money to start a business which was his one ambition, I sent him to his death."

For a long moment he stared at Peter and fought to control his mind; to free it from pain and unproductive hate, and channel it to the will for revenge. He concentrated on his day's work, and felt sanity begin to return.

His day had started with a memory. He had walked through the park for a while, trying to form his thoughts about the Carlin killing, and, as he watched the birds coming in across the lake, a memory had grown in his head. A memory from the past, long ago before the war in Africa; his camp up the Congo River, his bearers crooning round the fire, and, all around them, the forest. Then, out of the forest, a man had come crawling on his hand and knees.

The man was a half-caste named Eddie Windsor, which he might possibly have been christened, and he was dying. He was dying of syphilis and malaria and the lack of a desire to live. He died quickly, raving most of the time, but, during his few lucid moments, he told Mott a story.

Windsor had gone up river, some months ago, looking for a diamond pipe which probably never existed, and which he never found at any event. But, on his way back, he found a trail in the jungle. It was a fresh trail and, like a hyena, always ready for pickings, he followed it in the hope it might lead to something of value.

It didn't. All that trail led to was a smell. A terrible smell, worse, far worse than anything he had experienced before, and was made up of death and corruption and sheer terror.

And though Windsor was not a brave man, and his porters left him, he went on. He went on alone, following the trail and the smell, till at last the trail opened up into a little clearing and, in the centre of the clearing was a pit. It was a deep, deep pit, which might have been used as a trap for some large animal, but it wasn't. No animal would have gone near that hole in the ground with its terrible smell and the noises that came from it. The pit was full of people; scores of people. Most of them were dead, but a few still lived, and the living were trying to climb up out of the earth on the piled bodies of the dead.

Windsor could have helped them out of course. He could have lowered branches for them to climb on, or made a rope out of tendrils. He didn't, he ran. He ran as though his life depended on it, which it probably did.

And it wasn't fear of death or corruption which made him do that. He had seen them a score of times, and they wouldn't have moved him. It was the appearance of those people in the pit that frightened him; for they were like something out of a nightmare. Big Congo Negroes whose bodies should have been blue-black but weren't. Their skin was white—as white as snow.

Mott had disregarded the story of course. He had put it down to disease, wood alcohol and Windsor's dying mind. And, when Windsor did die, he forgot it. He forgot it completely till that morning, and then, all at once it came back to him, and a theory started to grow.

For could that half-caste's tale, told so long ago, have possibly been true? And, if it were true, might it just link up with the vague theory which was running through his head? For over an hour, he walked in the park, considering it. And then he went to work.

The work was dull at first. Work which he hated because it lay, not with action, but research; research on musty files in drab, government offices which held the records of the dead.

And, there were so many dead in his theory. The dead rich who had been born unloved and untalented, and craved for something to do with their lives. Lots and lots of the rich, and some of the poor too. The dead poor who had no capital, but a great burning ambition to find a backer and make good. Yes, a great army of the dead, stretching down through the years, and Susan Carlin and Devi Parbat might just be the last of them.

All day Mott had considered the dead and their stories as told by the files of the Records Office, while officials of the Sunday skeleton staff, well bribed to give him access, but grey as their ledgers, sat watching. And at last he had what he wanted, and walked back to Frenten Street, with the almost certain knowledge why Susan Carlin died; knowledge which he might never be able to prove.

Just as he had opened the door of the little office, the phone started to ring. He'd ignored it for a moment, staring round the room and wondering where Peter had gone; then he'd picked it up. He listened quite indifferently at first, expecting nothing of importance, and then, slowly, his face had altered and he'd heard Parbat dying.

Rage came. Rage which made him break and tear and destroy at random to blot out the memory of that dying voice on the phone. Rage which could only be sated by the thrown typewriter, the upturned files and a chair splintered against the wall. Rage that died as quickly as it had begun, and soon changed to guilt and grief and remorse. It took him a long time to shake off these emotions, but, at last he did, and settled down to tell Peter how Parbat died.

"I'm sorry, really so very sorry." Peter looked at the big man, trying to show what he felt, but there was just nothing left to say, only—"sorry." The Indian had given his life to help him, but words didn't mean anything now—only actions had meaning.

And, so far, all action had come from the other side. Susan was dead, because she had learned something she couldn't mention. Ethel Sommers and Parbat had gone down before a forty-five revolver, held by a person with the fingers of a freak and there was only one witness left

149

who might help him. One man who might be broken and might tell the truth.

Yes, they were all dead; Susan and Sommers and Parbat. And, unless he found the truth tonight, he might be finished too. Finished and done with. His picture in the papers and the hue and cry out for him. He leaned back against the wall and told Mott of his decision and the phone call to Toni Marric.

"Oh, yes, they know you're back all right. I saw the press this morning." Mott stared at him and he was trying to make up his mind.

"By now, I hoped that Parbat might have learned enough from Sommers for us to go to the police, but that's impossible, still impossible."

And, as he looked at Peter, he wanted to warn him. He wanted to tell him of his theory, that the records and the half-caste's story had brought to mind; the horrible story that Parbat's murder seemed to confirm. To tell Peter exactly what they were up against and that, if he kept his appointment with Marric, he would be meeting death as well.

But he didn't tell him. For, as he looked at Peter's tortured, not quite sane face, he knew that it was probably the only way out. He couldn't prove his theory and, without a bait, he might never prove it, and Parbat would go unavenged. He didn't want that, and, as he watched Peter, he saw how it could be, how it had been, so many times before.

Yes, he saw it just like that. The goat tied below the tree and, as dusk fell, the goat began to bleat in terror, and tug at its rope, and claw the ground in its efforts to escape from the thing in the shadows. And he watched from that tree. Then, into the clearing, came a yellow and black beast and he pulled the trigger and fired.

And now, if he were to avenge his friend, he would need another goat to entice a tiger. He got up and held out his hand to Peter.

"I see," he said. "You told Marric you would meet

him in an hour. Very well, it's your right and your decision. Go to him and make the blighter talk, and then come back and we'll contact the police. And, good luck, son, lots and lots of luck. As I told you before, I admire courage."

He watched the man he was probably sending to his death walk out of the room and, for a moment, he listened to his footsteps on the stairs. Then he picked up the cracked telephone from the floor and tried it. Quite miraculously, it still worked and he heard the dialing tone.

He smiled as his number rang, and his smile was confident, for he felt that he had to win. The goat was already on its way to the clearing, the tiger would not be far behind, and behind the tiger he would come. He would come, and he would bring a witness with him, and the matter would be finished, and Parbat not have died in vain.

He spoke briefly and authoritatively into the phone and, when he put it down, he looked at his watch. If he were to succeed, the timing had to be just right. Five minutes early and he would warn their enemies. A minute late and Peter Carlin would most certainly die. He tucked the watch back into his pocket and started to stand up. At that moment, the smile was wiped off his face and he knew he had failed. For he was no longer alone in the building.

The feet on the stairs were heavy and ponderous and he knew whose feet they were. The police had found Parbat's body with the address in his pocket, and they were coming to check on that address.

Mott had no fear of the police, but he couldn't afford the time. He had no time at all to spare, for every second he wasted was taking Peter a little nearer to his death. He drew back into the shadows behind the desk and knew he would have to fight.

The three policemen were big and heavy and filled with self-confidence and steak and two vegetables. They were City of London police, quite independent of the

Yard, and they had been sent round to Frenten Street by a phone call which gave few details of what they were to look for. They hadn't liked that at all.

And they didn't like what they saw in the office either. The broken typewriter, the chair shattered against the wall, and the papers and files strewn at random as though by a lunatic. And, above all, they didn't like the man. The big man, crouched in the corner, with the body of a gorilla, and a face that looked capable of murder.

"Yes, capable of anything," they thought, staring at the ruin around them. "Taken red-handed—caught in the act—guilty as hell." And, without a word being spoken they knew what they had to do.

They were old, tough cops, and each of them had been in a similar situation a score of times. They opened out, one in the centre of the room, one on each side, and then started to close in on the man, expecting him to draw back or try to slip past them. But they were wrong— quite wrong.

For the man didn't draw back, and he didn't try to escape. He just stood there, grim and silent, and waited for them. And, just before they reached him, he acted. He raised his hands, a roar like a battle-cry broke from his lips, and he came out fighting.

And, while Mott was fighting for time and Peter's life, a middle-aged woman in a faded, blue coat took one last look at Frenten Street and started to walk away.

She smiled slightly, as she walked, for she had done the job she was paid to do, and her superiors seemed satisfied. Peter Carlin was of no more interest to her and she was going home.

She neither knew nor cared that, in just over the hour, her work would cause the death of at least four people.

CHAPTER TEN

EIGHT o'clock of a quiet Sunday evening, a hint of rain and fog from the east, little traffic on the streets, and the lamps like oranges above the Cromwell Road. Peter Carlin driving a stolen car towards the people who had killed his wife.

Peter drove fast at first. The noise of the engine did a little to dull the pounding of his heart, and he wanted to put distance between the car and the embankment where he had found it. Not too fast though; however important time might seem, he could risk no brush with the traffic police. Already Hammersmith and Chiswick Bridge had passed and he slowed down and switched on the radio.

"The poetry of Rainer Maria Rilke," said a warbling voice from the Third Programme (he pronounced, the word "pourtery") "deals in images and dreams which might well be described as the 'suchness' of the human psyche." Peter punched the button hurriedly and was rewarded with Vera Lynn rendering Lilli Marlene for the lads and lasses of an army reunion.

He was in Richmond now, driving among narrow, but well-lit streets, and bright shop windows, and suddenly there was a policeman's arm coming up at a crossroad. He braked sharply and watched a big Cadillac turn out of the side street.

Such a nice Caddy too; this year's model, with smoky blue paint the colour of Turkish Delight, rows of winking lights, and a uniformed chauffeur edging her gently round the bend. Yes, a nice car; a rich man's pet, an executive's front, with two quiet figures sitting beside the driver and another figure almost lying across the thick cushions of the back seat.

So, why should he stare so hard at her as the policeman's arm went down and the road cleared? Why did he scream his engine to overtake, and lean out to try and catch a glimpse of that still figure in the back?

For it was impossible of course. It had to be impossible. It was just a trick of light and shadow and the way two bodies were hinged together. He couldn't see the man's face, which was hidden by a magazine, but it must be imagination. It must be, because the one he thought he recognized was miles away—a thousand miles away. And fear, when he found it, would not be in any bright Richmond Street, but at the dark cottage where Susan died. This was just some tired tycoon driving out to a pleasant house near Guilford and the "stock-broker country."

He pushed all thoughts of recognition from his mind and stepped hard on the accelerator. The car shot ahead towards Kingston with its tyres screaming, and he tried to concentrate on Miss Lynn's gay, reassuring voice.

And behind him, far behind soon, quiet and slow, with her engine barely ticking over, for there was no hurry, the big Cadillac followed. A nice car, such a nice car, with the stars winking on her Turkish-Delight paint, and the banks of lights before her, and her owner stretched out on the back seat.

A quiet little man, her owner. He sat alone in the back, turning the pages of his magazine, and hiding thoughts which weren't at all quiet, as one after another, the milestones crept by, and the car carried him deeper into Surrey. Death on a pale blue horse, riding to Reigate.

And suddenly Peter was almost there. He hadn't thought about it till that moment; just kept his mind on the way he was going to deal with Toni Marric, but not really considered the end of the journey. But this was almost the end and soon he would be talking to the man who knew the name of Susan's killer.

There were signs coming up on the road now. Private signs at first, extolling somebody's beer, somebody's home-grown tomatoes, somebody's pedigreed cocker spaniels. And then the official signs reading STEEP HILL—ROAD JUNCTION—DANGEROUS TO CYCLISTS. For a moment his headlights seemed to hang over the void, and then he drove down the hill into the town.

It seemed an early-to-bed town, with nobody in the streets but lights in most of the windows. Good, strong lights behind gay curtains which reminded him of warm things; double beds and baths and last-thing-at-night drinks and slippers by the fire. There was suddenly a great longing in his eyes as he looked at the warm lights of Reigate. Then he drove on towards the coldness that awaited him.

As always, he nearly missed the side turning; it was so sudden, so unexpected from the main road. A lane cut deep in the flank of the hill, with clay walls much higher than a car, and stunted thorn trees on the walls which seem to be clutching downwards. He drove slowly up its long half-mile and, at the end, where the gash in the hillside fanned out, stood the cottage.

Toni Marric had kept his appointment. Drawn up in front of the door was a black Ford Consul, one of the work's cars probably and possibly, just possibly, the same car which had driven Susan to her death. He parked his own car in front of it and opened the door. As he stepped out, he seemed to be leaving not a car, but the world too —the whole stupid, brutal, but sometimes warm world— for the cold domain of the devil.

And for the first time, he realized what his meeting, what his phone call might mean. For if Mott was right, if Toni Marric was merely a pawn in the hands of an organization, would he have come alone to the cottage? Would it not have been more natural for him to have contacted Susan's killers and brought them too?

But alone or not, it seemed that Toni had a key. The cottage door was open and Toni stood framed on the step, trying to grin as he walked towards him. Somebody who had been Toni Marric that was; for he had changed.

Peter recognized the shape of the head and the stance

155

of the body, but that was all he did recognize. It was a stranger who stood before him and tried to smile with a face that couldn't smile. A stranger who took his hand in a grip which was as soft and damp as something which had died years ago under water.

And the stranger wasn't as Mott had described him, hard and murderous and held up by cocaine. There was no drug in that twitching body now and only its memory held him up. He followed the creature that had once been Marric into the cottage and there was something like pity fighting the fear and anger in his eyes.

The room inside was unaltered. The same oak refectory table stood before him with candles burning on it, as the light must have been disconnected. His golf clubs leaned in the corner and the same faded curtain separated lounge from dining room. And as he looked at that curtain, he knew that his fears were right. For Toni Marric had not come alone.

Yes, though that curtain might look the same, there was something different about it. It was folded. Just where the ends met, there was a fold with something holding them apart. Something which he had never completely believed in, but which told him that Susan's diary and Parbat's dying words spoke the exact truth.

Yes, they had told the truth, for there was a hand on that curtain. A hand which he had never seen before, because it was the left, and had always been hidden by darkness, gloves or a pocket.

And that hand might have been recognized on the wheel of a speeding car, for it was deformed. It had killed Susan and Parbat and probably a score of others, but it still looked oddly pathetic against the faded cloth. The fingers were broad as a man's but short as a child's. They had only one joint and the nails grew where the knuckles should have been.

And, beside him, Toni Marric was trying to speak. He took his time about it, mouthing for words that wouldn't come, while the sweat ran down his face, and his breath was sour acid mingling with the candle smoke. And, when he did speak, it was in a voice that Peter had never heard before.

"Sorry," he said in that strange broken voice. "I had to do it, Pete, but—sorry—so terribly sorry." Then he turned and shut the door behind him.

And, as soon as the door was properly closed, the curtains parted, and the man who had killed Susan came into the room.

Sir Walter Rayne leaned back against the table, with his deformed hand resting on the wood, and the candle light glowing on his face. And it was a good face too, with deep, carved lines that came from responsibility, and belief in his purpose, and strength; such a lot of strength. Enough strength to kill a daughter.

But he didn't smile, as Peter feared he might, almost dreaded that he might; because there was something obscene in the thought of that cold face smiling. No, he didn't smile, for he had no part with anything as vulgar as mirth or humour or conventional warmth.

And, as he watched Rayne's face, Peter seemed to take it in for the first time—to look right through the hero's mask, the chiselled, saintly flesh, and see the tiger muzzle behind it. For, though Rayne was an aristocrat, he was something else. Something which no women ever are, except in legend, and very few men. He was a completely solitary human being; a cat who above everything wants to walk by itself.

As he looked at him, Shelley's description of another aristocrat ran through his head. "I met Murder in the way—he had a mask like Castlereagh."

"So, you really did get back, my boy," said Walter Rayne. "You got home all the way from Russia. Please let me congratulate you." His voice was as beautiful as ever; a tuned instrument which had taken centuries to perfect and polish.

Two men had followed him into the room and Peter recognized them. Their names were Martin and Wade, and one was his chauffeur and the other a general facto-

157

tum. They stood stiffly behind their master and they were like soldiers guarding a reigning monarch. Their faces were carved granite, showing no emotion at all.

"Yes, it was clever of you to get out, Mr. Carlin. Clever and brave and, on the surface, lucky. Which makes it a pity—such a great pity."

He broke off for a moment and seemed to be examining the nails of his horrid, little hand.

"Yes, it's a pity. Before my accident, I used to hunt two or three times a week but the end of a chase often sickened me. Though not a squeamish or even a merciful man, I felt that a gallant animal who had given good sport should have a chance. I never liked the practice of digging earths or driving the fox out with terriers, though of course they are necessary.

"I still feel that way, Mr. Carlin, and so I'm sorry about you. I'm sorry, that after your long and dangerous journey from Russia, I must be responsible for your death."

"Yes, I suppose you will be." There was no surprise or fear in Peter's voice, just curiosity. He watched the tiger muzzle through Rayne's face, and knew that he had killed Susan and Parbat and, probably many, many others. He had to know why though. He had to look right through to the soul, if he had one, to see what drove him on— what made him tick.

"You'll kill me, Sir Walter, just as you killed your own daughter. And, though I don't know why, though I don't know what mania or devil drives you on, I think I know something else. I think you're already frying in hell for it."

"Good, Mr. Carlin, very good. As I said, I like an animal that gives a gallant fight." Rayne didn't smile but his eyebrows raised slightly over the thin, pale forehead.

"I have to kill you for a very simple reason. You are in my way. Just as a rather silly girl with an unhealthy conscience got in my way. It seems only fair, however, that I tell you why you must die."

And he told him. He told him slowly and patiently, as though explaining an important lesson to a child. He told his story without hiding anything or seeking to justify himself. He didn't have to, for, to him, his actions seemed the most natural in the world. And, though Peter knew the end of the story would be his death, he stood still and listened fascinated.

It was the story of a family, and the family went back through the centuries of English history. A story of pillage and conquest and always taking but never giving.

For Saxon house-carl went down before Norman horsemen and the men who were nothing became rich. Then the grey or red castles went up and the conquest was achieved, and the horsemen became knights, but it didn't stop the horsemen. They went on riding for themselves. They rode into Scotland and Wales and Ireland, searching for power, and each mile they rode, each century they lived, made them a little more of a law to themselves.

And, when times changed, and there was no more land left to conquer, the Rayne family didn't alter and they didn't stop. The fighting ships sailed out for gold and glory, and other ships that cared little for glory took chained black savages to a new life in the New World.

So, year after year, century by century, the Raynes became richer and richer, and more powerful, and more convinced that the world was theirs to do what they liked with. And fields were enclosed, and children died in their northern mines, and money poured in from every corner of the earth.

Then one day, the earth altered, and the sands started to run out. They ran out before ideas, and the ideas carried dangerous slogans such as "Liberty," "Equality," "Fraternity"—"The greatest Happiness for the Greatest Number" and "Jack is as good as his Master." And those ideas finished the Raynes, or nearly finished them.

At the turn of the century, three heirs died in quick succession, and land tax, and estate tax, and death duties, gnawed like rats into the wealth centuries had built up. Then, one by one, the big houses fell empty, the sale signs went up over the carved gateways and the grass grew in the yards where horsemen had mounted. And, at the end, only the house at Steynnings was left.

But there was a boy who loved that house. He was a strange boy, perhaps a throw-back to another age, and his hand made him a mockery to other children. He wandered alone through the grounds and the long, dark corridors and, in his imagination, he seemed to see the house as a dream castle, secure and embattled against the outside world.

And, when he was still quite young, he learned that he was going to lose it. He listened to his father, a grey, broken man without any of the family fire in him, and he heard of taxes and crippling debt, and the need to move with the times and accept defeat.

But the boy didn't believe in defeat. He left the grey man and walked through the long gallery, between pictures of robber baron and iron-master, cavalier and privateer, and one ancestor with a hand like his who had lost it at Waterloo; all the "takers" of the world.

And among those painted dead he knew that he would have to fight for his home. To fight for it with every means in his power against the forces outside; the rats, the under-dogs, the little people, who wished to steal it from him.

He fought all right. As soon as his father died, and the debts and taxes and unpaid mortgages became his, he started to fight. And, because he had a gimmick, a new idea, he won.

"It is easier for a camel to go through the eye of a needle than for a rich man to enter the Kingdom of God." Though he didn't believe the saying himself, many of the rich seemed to, and that showed him the way to build a business.

For, when the first stroke comes, the first heart attack, how many of the rich will begin to consider their past lives, and dread death, and begin to store up treasures in heaven? "A thousand pounds to this charity," they write in their wills, "ten thousand to that." They set it down well and legally and forget the widowed cousin who lives out at Tooting taking in boarders, the scapegrace nephew with the failing motor showrooms on the Great West Road.

And, as Walter Rayne considered this, he saw something which puzzled him. The fact that many people who have spent their entire lives producing or hoarding money, towards the end, will part with it graciously in the name of the Great God Charity. And he realized his business, his vocation; a way to direct some of that money into his own hands.

So it began. His old, respected name went down at the head of a dozen good causes, a hundred appeals for funds. And, in time, those causes not only bore his name but were controlled and governed by him, and their accounts were open to him alone and those he appointed to serve him.

And the money came in, for soon he was a legend, a symbol of all that is good in British aristocracy. His was the quiet, sad figure with the banker's draft who stepped into the rosewood bedroom and smiled at the maiden lady who coughed, oh, so gently, on the pillow. His was the stern, authoritative figure walking down the companionway of a private yacht to the dying financier fighting his blocked liver. Sir Walter Rayne—the Saint.

Much of the money did go to charity of course. It had to for the sake of publicity and the sake of the books. The appeals he made were for genuine causes and genuine needs, but they didn't take everything, not nearly everything. All the time there was a stream of money into his own account and the debts were paid off, the roof at Steynnings was repaired, and the gardeners and servants and painters came back.

And, one day, he was able to look up at the pictures in the gallery and know he had kept his promise.

It didn't stop there of course. He couldn't have stopped, even had he wanted to. What began as fraudulent conversion to salvage a house had grown to a joy, and obsession and, at last, a personal war against the world; a war of deceit and fraud which ended in murder.

161

And the money kept coming in. More charities were founded, prospered for a time, and then died from lack of funds. And, once or twice, a suspicious benefactor died, too, a little earlier than he should have done.

For, though Rayne started on his own, he soon took on helpers. Not only Martin and Wade, believers like himself in a past age, who had been born to serve and followed him as the men at arms of a feudal baron, but other people too. Men and women who spoke little of their past and had no dream of family greatness; only the dreams of money urged them on.

These people worked for him and were paid by him and, after a time, might almost have worked without pay. For, though they would never admit it, as they sat in their clubs and road-houses and saloon bars, there was something in Rayne's face they had to call "master."

So his schemes grew and prospered and spread far wider than their intended beginnings. The almshouses at Glasgow, for instance, supported by charity, but drawing high rents from ex-convicts who paid not in cash but in service. The leper colony in the Congo; twelve thousand a year guaranteed subscription, but no hospital. Only a reception centre, a transit camp, from which the sick, well counted and well documented, were marched out through hidden trails to a row of deep pits in the jungle.

And there were other business interests too, which had nothing to do with charity. The brothel in Liverpool, the receiver's den at Antwerp, a private yacht, based in the Solent, which now and again brought strange cargoes from the south. All the spreading pockets of a resurrected empire at war against the world; an empire from the Dark Ages, whose dream was "Might is Right," "What I Have I Hold," and mailed horsemen riding under the Rayne banners through a burning village.

All this he told to Peter, and he told it without shame or guilt, as though his acts were right and proper and quite natural. And, as he watched that cold, mad, but not quite mad face, Peter knew what he was dealing with. For, in his foul way, this man was a patriot. He fought to preserve an England he believed in. He stood quite still and listened to the end of Rayne's story.

"And then, a disgraced servant got in my way, Mr. Carlin. She was a woman called Molly Sommers who had once been in my employ. She found out certain facts about me and tried to profit from them by blackmailing my daughter. Fortunately I was informed about this and was able to put an end to her."

His hand contracted slightly as he spoke, and Peter imagined how it might have looked on the wheel of a car while something like a bundle of rags rolled before it.

"The damage was done, however, for Susan knew the truth. And Susan was a strange girl, it seemed. There were two actions open to her and I could have understood either of them. She could have comprehended and accepted my actions, or told you and gone to the police.

"Yes, either way would have been understandable but Susan did neither. There is insanity on her grandmother's side of the family and she must have inherited it. She could neither betray me or realize what I fought for. Her mind just started to wither."

"And so you decided to kill her?" Peter stared at him and, for the first time, he saw something like sorrow in his eyes. For Walter Rayne could have forgiven his daughter anything—anything except weakness.

"No, not at the beginning, though I prepared for her death. I planned it thoroughly from the night I saw her at your flat. I prepared for everything; even for a scapegoat who could never return to defend himself.

"I never wanted to kill her though. You must believe that, Carlin. She was both a threat and an embarrassment for me and I saw her mind growing into something small and ignoble, just as my mother's had done. But I didn't want to kill her. Even at the end I never wanted that."

"Yes, I believe you." Peter watched Rayne's face and he saw how it must have been, just as Mott had thought it had been. The trip to Russia arranged with Marric weeks before; another car substituted for his; and his own car, with a false wheel to protect the prints, driving

Susan down to Surrey; his gun fired once with a pair of pliers, and another gun held in that small, crippled hand. Then there had been the false statements of the maid and Toni Marric and the matter was finished. Susan was dead and he was buried alive.

"No," said Rayne. "No, I didn't want to kill my daughter. On the night you left for Russia, I'd arranged to call for her. I wanted to make one last appeal to her loyalty, her sanity. We drove round in the car for hours and I tried to make her see the truth—to understand that my actions were right—to realize that our blood was above the condemnation of the herd and the gutter.

"And she couldn't—so I shot her! I shot my daughter down and she couldn't face death at the end. She struggled with me and tried to fight her way out of the car. I had to shoot her through the back of the head like any coward."

"Poor, poor Susan." Peter turned away from the man at the table and his own approaching death meant nothing to him. All he could see was the picture of his wife's face at the window of the car and her hands clawing at the door handle and a gun coming up behind her.

"Yes, my poor Susan," he said. Then he looked at the other man in the corner of the room. Toni Marric crouched in that corner as though he wanted to hide in it.

"And you, Toni. Why did you lie, I wonder? Why did you help him?" He watched the slack mouth trying to speak, but it was Rayne who answered.

"Mr. Marric lied for a very simple reason, Carlin. He was paid to. For Mr. Marric is a strange man, you know. He has no warmth, no loyalty, no depth of human feeling, but a single great love—the love of his work. I'd known that for some time and I thought we might help each other, Mr. Marric and I.

"As soon as I had made my decision, I called on Marric and I made him an offer. A new workshop, new machines, all the things he wanted, for one little lie and the price of your life. And Marric never loved you, Carlin.

You were always in his way, holding back his schemes and experiments. The practical businessman, frustrating and creator." Rayne stared at the man in the corner and Peter saw Toni Marric raise his hands to cover his face.

"Of course, Mr. Marric didn't accept my offer at once," said Rayne. "That would have been expecting too much and he was frightened. I had to give him courage before we did business. Lots of courage which comes out of a hypodermic syringe. After that he wasn't frightened any more and he became my man. Just as Martin and Wade here and many, many others, are my men.

"Yes, Marric lied because I told him to and Susan's maid lied because I said so and you were all washed up, as the saying goes. You see, you were the obvious choice for a fall guy, a scapegoat, though I'm sorry about it now. You've shown yourself a gallant animal in getting back from Russia and I like that, I like it very much indeed."

He turned and walked to the back of the room; a tall, erect figure on oddly cat-like feet, with his little hand gripping the table as he moved round it.

"Yes, I'm sorry, Peter," he said. And it was the first time he had used the Christian name.

"I'm sorry it has to be this way, but I must protect a dream. My dream of greatness and power and nobility— a thousand years of being great, brought down by the small and the weak and the contemptible.

"And now the story telling's done and Wade is going to kill you."

The man called Wade came from behind the table and his hand was like leather round a big, out-dated revolver. His face was a Saxon's face, the face of a serf who obeyed orders—any orders.

For men like Wade had died in a hundred lost causes because they were told to. They had stood unflinching at Hastings because Harold wanted them to. They had charged up the Valley of Death with the Five Hundred because Cardigan ordered them to. They had marched on Conquered Bridge because a German king willed it.

Wade's was the face of the uncomplaining, the follower, the soldier who obeyed orders and never asked the reason why.

And his hand would obey orders too. The hard, brown hand of a gamekeeper, a ghillie; about to kill an animal at its master's command. A hand which didn't think, but knew its job.

Peter stood quite still watching the big Webley swing round and, for a moment, he thought of fighting; of hurling himself on Wade and trying to tear it from him. The same instant he knew it was useless. This man was a killer, as professional as any Chicago gunman, and he would be dead before he reached the barrel.

No, there was no point in fighting, and no point in cursing Rayne either; cursing and reviling him for his daughter's murder, or his insane pride, or his crippled hand. This was the end of the line, the last lap of the journey and it was better, far better, to face it with dignity. He stood still and watched death in that brown finger growing white on the trigger.

And it was a pity he did that and looked so fixedly forward. For, once again, as on the road from Pushkin Village, he never saw the miracle that saved him.

Behind his back the door opened. Gregor Radek lifted his machine pistol and blew Wade's head off.

Radek came into the room with the gun on his hip and he sprayed that room as a gardener sprays roses. He tore Martin's body to red ruin as he scrabbled for the revolver that Wade had dropped, and he sent a long burst at the tall man who stood behind the table. Then he lowered his arm, leaned back against the wall and began to wipe his face with a handkerchief. A small neat figure, doing the job he was paid to do, a job which had just killed three men.

But one man did not die—not at once. Sir Walter Rayne still stood on his feet, which he shouldn't have done, for there was a hole in his chest you could put a hand through. His face showed more hatred than Peter had ever seen. It was the hatred of the strong brought down by the weak, the lion at bay, the tiger held by a thin, puny trap.

For a long moment that blaze of hate lit up his lined, parchment face and then it went out and there was just bewilderment there. Bewilderment and doubt and thoughts running through his head saying—"this can't be"—"this hasn't happened"—"no, it couldn't happen to me for I am above death."

And then his knees started to buckle, his eyes glazed and he sank down with the final realization on his face—"but, by God, it has happened."

Then he died. He died on the floor beside Martin and Wade and his blood mingled with theirs and in death master and man were not divided.

"Well, my friend, I seem to have arrived in the nick of time, as the English say." Radek tucked away the handkerchief and his fingers stroked the barrel of the Thompson gun.

"Yes, just in time, Mr. Carlin, but don't move, please. Don't move a muscle. After such a long chase, I have no wish to kill you but, if it's necessary, I shall. You are of little importance to us now, and that's the one we really want, I fancy." He motioned to the two men who had come into the room with him and they walked forward to Toni Marric.

"Yes, I've come a long way on your behalf, Mr. Carlin. My superiors were inclined to blame me for your lucky escape and, knowing as you did our interrogation methods, it seemed necessary for you to die.

"Our people over here have been watching you since you arrived at Dover. I had hoped that they would finish the job for me, but they are a cautious lot. A most unpleasant man at the embassy insisted I should come over and attend to you myself. He also said that, if you were to die, it must be done in a way that would throw no suspicion on the Soviet Government.

"Quite frankly I was worried. I thought you would go straight to the British police and the story would come out. Fortunately that did not happen. You decided to play detective and made a phone call one of our agents overheard. And so here I am. In for the death, as you say." He turned away from Peter and looked at the piled bodies on the floor.

"And you found your wife's killers, it seems. One day I will be interested to hear the story, but not just now. Now we have work to do. Now I have the one I really want, the prime mover, the inventor of this rocket device I hoped you would tell me about.

"Yes, Mr. Carlin, it's starting all over again, I'm afraid, and I am not going to kill you. I am going to try and take you and Mr. Marric back to Russia and there we will hear the full story from his own lips." Radek glanced through the open doorway behind him. Outside it was pitch dark, with a small cluster of lights in the distance; the warm friendly lights of Reigate.

"And do you really think you'll get away with it?" Peter stared at the man who had just saved his life. In a way, he would have preferred death from Wade's gun.

"I don't really know, Mr. Carlin. I honestly haven't the slightest idea." Radek watched his assistants handcuff Peter and Marric together and smiled; the thin, patient smile of an employee who did a routine job and expected nothing except his wages.

"No, I rather doubt if I'll succeed and I've heard your police are efficient. We'll soon know just how efficient." There was the same prim look on his face that Peter had seen in Leningrad.

"You see, I don't matter much, Mr. Carlin. Only the department that I work for matters. I could kill you both now and get away, but I won't if I can help it. I am expendable and, if I can get you back, it would be to the advantage of my department. Yes, I am going to try and earn my very generous salary." He drew back to let Peter and Marric pass in front of him.

"And now let's go, shall we? Let's try and find out just how good your police really are. Let's see if they can stop me taking you home."

They pushed Peter through the door, and they were taking him back to Russia and everything would start all over again. Mott was in London, still dazed and shattered by Parbat's death, the police had no idea as to where he was and Toni Marric was a weeping weight on his arm making escape impossible. There was no hope left. All that was left was Radek standing before the cottage and the memory of Radek's office; the animal pictures on the walls and a man who had once been a Nazi torturer coming through the doorway. That man was dead but doubtless there were many more like him.

He watched Radek walk to the end of the cottage, take a whistle from his pocket and blow two short blasts on it. From far off down the lane, an engine started and the Cadillac they had left there came to fetch them.

Yes, the Cadillac was coming and it was not a car to Peter but a hearse, a tumbril, a prison van to take him back to hell. Round the bend it came, with its engine a purr and the side lights winking at him. A lovely car—four thousand pounds worth of car—the sweet chariot "comin' for to carry him home."

And now Radek was stopping it. Like a car park attendant, he was waving instructions to draw it up before the cottage. He was lifting his hand to stop it just where he wanted. No, by God, he wasn't!

Radek wasn't waving to the car now, he was shaking his fist at it. He was shouting in a fury and drawing back before it. And, all at once, Peter knew that the nightmare was over and he was free.

For the Cadillac didn't stop, it came on. It came on in a sudden rush, with the exhaust a scream to the hills behind it, and white tyres scattering gravel, and headlamps blazing out to silhouette Radek like a puppet on a stage. Four thousand pounds of steel, glass and alloy rushing to destroy themselves against the cottage wall.

It was over in a second, but it seemed to take a year. He saw Radek begin to raise his gun and the same moment realize that it was too late. He saw him start to move aside and know that that was useless too. And, at the very end, he saw Radek smile. One final, prim, old maid's smile; the last gesture of someone who had done the job to the best of his ability and has no fear in him.

And, just before the car reached that wall, Peter heard something he would remember till his dying day. A familiar sound but amplified a thousand times. A sound like a beetle's body being crushed against glass.

CHAPTER ELEVEN

THEY had cleared up the mess and removed the bodies. They had taken the surviving Russians to London and Toni Marric to hospital. Mr. Mott was delighted with himself.

For the business was finished at last and Parbat had been avenged. His was a good death and it was paid for now. His killers had been destroyed by a Russian police chief and the Russian was dead too. For it was he, Moldon Mott, who had the last word. His had been the final triumph.

He lolled back in the one comfortable chair in the police station and he thought about that triumph. The fight in Parbat's office, which had held him back. The dash to Reigate, and the Cadillac found parked in the lane.

He hadn't expected that, of course, never foreseen that the Russians would have taken a hand, but he put two and two together and acted. The chauffeur dragged from his seat and throttled on the ground, the car creeping forward as the whistle sounded and, at last, Radek's body like an elastic doll dancing in the headlights.

Yes, Mr. Mott was well pleased. He stretched out his legs, lit a cigarette and beamed at his audience: Peter Carlin, Sir Thomas Winterton of the Yard, Colonel Salter from Intelligence, and a dour inspector of police, named McDoggart. His smile was wide and friendly but still modest. The smile of a young Lindbergh before the Paris crowds, a magnanimous conqueror accepting the keys to a defeated city.

"Well, that's about it, gentlemen. As soon as I remembered that half-caste's yarn, I got a clue. One of Rayne's pet charities was a leper colony and it seemed to tie up. A few hours at the Records Office confirmed my suspicions. Too many people had willed money to his charities and too many had died soon afterwards. I was on to him at once after that and, if Mr. Carlin hadn't lost his head and your people not interfered, it would have been settled much more tidily. Not that I'm blaming anyone, of course. Though not apparent to a normal mind, the story was quite obvious to someone who . . ." He coughed modestly and turned his smile towards Winterton.

Winterton did not smile back. He was too busy to smile for he was remembering. He was remembering a pleasant dinner at his club and how it had ended. First a telephone call from a man he thoroughly disliked, and then that man had come bursting into the restaurant. He had come in with his coat torn and blood running down the side of his face and he had almost dragged him out to the street.

And then that man had driven him down to Surrey. He had driven fast and badly, without care or consideration for other road users and he had kept looking at the clock and cursing vilely, but giving no explanation of his outrageous conduct.

And, at last, they had stopped in a side turning behind a big American car and Mott had got out and made, what seemed, an unprovoked attack on the driver.

The end was past thinking about. He, a senior official of the British police had been bundled into the Cadillac and made to witness murder against the wall of a cottage.

"Mr. Mott," he said, striving to keep his voice normal. "Just what sort of man do you think you are?"

"What sort of man?" If possible, Mott's smile became even wider and more self-satisfied. "I'd prefer not to give my opinion, Sir Thomas, but the facts should speak for themselves. The proof of the pudding is in the eating, eh? By their fruits ye shall know them."

"Aye, jest so—by their fruits." The policeman, McDoggart, had reached the end of endurance and he broke in before his superior could reply.

"And, what are those fruits, Mr. Mott? If I may, I'd like to give my opinion of this very sorry affair.

"In the first place, Mr. Carlin was considered guilty of his wife's murder because he seemed to have fled to Russia to avoid arrest. Very luckily he was able to escape and return home. I have nothing but admiration for him till then, but what does he do afterwards. He returns to his flat, hoping to find his wife's diary, and there he meets you. He meets you, falls under your influence, and together you decide to play detectives." He ignored the strangling sound that burst from Mott's lips and went on.

"Oh, no, I don't blame Mr. Carlin too much. After his experiences, his mind may well have been unhinged, and he neglected the obvious fact that it was his duty to give himself up to the police. No, as far as we are concerned, Mr. Carlin is free to leave when he wishes.

"But, as for you, Mr. Mott." His pencil tapped sharply on the desk as he spoke. "For you, there is no excuse. It was your duty as a citizen to contact the police, but it never occurred to you, did it? Aye, I admit that you may have stumbled on the truth in the end, but at what price? The price of six people's lives and the risk of Mr. Carlin's . . ."

"Why, you . . . halfpenny policeman!" Mott had regained speech now, though his face was a crimson lamp. "You dare to speak to me like this, you miserable bungler who couldn't detect a flea crawling on your own wretched back. To me, who has solved the case for you. You say it was I who risked Carlin's life when it was his own foolishness, and the fact that three stupid bobbies came and attacked me at Parbat's office, taking up valuable time. How dare you, man?"

But McDoggart did dare. He looked quite unabashed

by Mott's outburst, and there was a sour and slightly sadistic expression on his face as he went on.

"Aye, Mr. Mott, and thank you for reminding me. Three policemen sent to that office and assaulted by you in the execution of their duty. Seriously assaulted, according to the latest hospital reports. Very badly beaten about indeed.

"British law won't stand for that, Mr. Mott. British law protects the police officer against the hooligan. Aye, a very serious view, I expect the magistrates will take. There are penalties and punishments for that sort of behaviour." He licked his lips and there was great pleasure in his eyes as he pronounced the words.

Peter didn't wait for Mott's next outburst to subside. He would have liked to go over and support him, to thank him, but this wasn't the time and Mott didn't seem in need of help. He was standing in the middle of the room, abusing McDoggart, and he looked quite capable of taking care of himself. Mott, eccentricities and all, was hotly and violently *of* the world as Rayne had never been. Peter smiled slightly, raised his hand in salute, and went out.

And outside it was already morning. The spring sun was coming up over the Surrey hills and the rain and fog had blown away. He looked at those hills and, in the distance, he could just make out the little dot which was a cottage where a man had died for his dream of greatness and glory. It was such a little dot now and seemed far away in space and time, because he had other things to think about.

For Susan was really dead at last. She was dead and avenged and the story was finished and she could sleep in peace in the family vault.

He had to go on though. He had to go on because, however much he had once loved Susan, he was still alive and the world was his and there was nothing more to run away from. He walked out through the thin, morning sunlight to the car that would take him to London.